I0656655

Eugene Field

The house

an episode in the lives of Reuben Baker, astronomer, and of his wife Alice

Eugene Field

The house
an episode in the lives of Reuben Baker, astronomer, and of his wife Alice

ISBN/EAN: 9783742894366

Manufactured in Europe, USA, Canada, Australia, Japa

Cover: Foto ©Raphael Reischuk / pixelio.de

Manufactured and distributed by brebook publishing software
(www.brebook.com)

Eugene Field

The house

BY EUGENE FIELD

The House.

The Love Affairs of a Bibliomaniac.

A Little Book of Profitable Tales.

A Little Book of Western Verse.

Second Book of Verse.
> Each, 1 vol., 16mo, $1.25.

A Little Book of Profitable Tales
> Cameo Edition with etched portrait. 16mo. $1 25

Echoes from the Sabine Farm.
> 4to, $2.00.

With Trumpet and Drum.
> 16mo, $1.00.

Love-Songs of Childhood.
> 16mo, $1.00.

The House

The Chapters in this Book

		PAGE
I	WE BUY A PLACE	1
II	OURSELVES AND OUR NEIGHBORS	14
III	WE MAKE OUR BARGAIN KNOWN	23
IV	THE FIRST PAYMENT	34
V	WE NEGOTIATE A MORTGAGE	45
VI	I AM BESOUGHT TO BUY THINGS	57
VII	OUR PLANS FOR IMPROVEMENTS	68
VIII	THE VANDALS BEGIN THEIR WORK	77
IX	NEIGHBOR MACLEOD'S THISTLE	89
X	COLONEL DOLLER'S GREAT IDEA	99
XI	I MAKE A STAND FOR MY RIGHTS	110
XII	I AM DECEIVED IN MR. WAX	121
XIII	EDITOR WOODSIT A TRUE FRIEND	132
XIV	THE VICTIM OF AN ORDINANCE	143
XV	THE QUESTION OF INSURANCE	154
XVI	NEIGHBOR ROBBINS' PLATYPUS	165
XVII	OUR DEVICES FOR ECONOMIZING	175
XVIII	I STATE MY VIEWS ON TAXATION	185
XIX	OTHER PEOPLE'S DOGS	195
XX	I ACQUIRE POISON AND EXPERIENCE	205
XXI	WITH PLUMBERS AND PAINTERS	215
XXII	THE BUTLER'S PANTRY	226
XXIII	ALICE'S NIGHT WATCHMAN	237
XXIV	DRIVEWAYS AND WALL-PAPERS	248
XXV	AT LAST WE ENTER OUR HOUSE	258

WE BUY A PLACE

IT was either Plato the Athenian, or Confucius the Chinese, or Andromachus the Cretan — or some other philosopher whose name I disremember — that remarked once upon a time, and the time was many centuries ago, that no woman was happy until she got herself a home. It really makes no difference who first uttered this truth, the truth itself is and always has been recognized as one possessing nearly all the virtues of an axiom.

I recall that one of the first wishes I heard Alice express during our honeymoon was that we should sometime be rich enough to be able to build a dear little house for ourselves. We were poor, of course; otherwise our air castle would not have been "a dear little house"; it would have been a palatial residence with a dance-hall at the top and a wine-cellar at the bottom thereof. I have always observed that when the money comes in the poetry flies out. Bread and cheese and kisses are all well enough for poverty-stricken romance, but as soon as a poor man receives a windfall his thoughts turn inevitably to a contemplation of the probability of terrapin and canvasbacks.

I encouraged Alice in her fond day-dreaming, and we decided between us that the dear little house should be a cottage, about which the roses and the honeysuckles should clamber in summer, and which in winter should be banked up with straw and leaves, for Alice and I were both of New England origin. I must confess that we had some reason for indulging these pleasing speculations, for at that time my Aunt Susan was living, and she was reputed as rich as mud (whatever that may mean), and this simile was by her neighbors coupled with another, which represented Aunt Susan as being as close as a clapboard on a house. Whatever her reputation was, I happened to be Aunt Susan's nearest of kin, and although I never

so far lost my presence of mind as to intimate even indirectly that I had any expecta-
tions, I wrote regularly to Aunt Susan once
a month, and every fall I sent her a box of
game, which I told her I had shot in the woods
near our boarding-house, but which actually
I had bought of a commission merchant in
South Water Street.

With the legacy which we were to receive
from Aunt Susan, Alice and I had it all fixed
up that we should build a cottage like one
which Alice had seen one time at Sweet
Springs while convalescing at that fashionable Missouri watering-place from an attack
of the jaundice. This cottage was, as I
was informed, an ingenious combination of
Gothic decadence and Norman renaissance
architecture. Being somewhat of an anti-
quarian by nature, I was gratified by the
promise of archaism which Alice's picture
of our future home presented. We picked
out a corner lot in, — well, no matter where:
that delectable dream, with its Gothic and
Norman features, came to an untimely end
all too soon. At its very height Aunt Susan
up and died, and a fortnight later we learned

that, after bequeathing the bulk of her property to foreign missions, she had left me,
whom she had condescended to refer to as
her "beloved nephew," nine hundred dollars in cash and her favorite flower-piece in
wax, a hideous thing which for thirty years
had occupied the corner of honor in the front
spare chamber.

I do not know what Alice did with the
wax-flowers. As for the nine hundred dollars, I appropriated it to laudable purposes.
Some of it went for a new silk dress for Alice;
the rest I spent for books, and I recall my
thrill of delight when I saw ensconced upon
my shelves a splendid copy of Audubon's
"Birds" with its life-size pictures of turkeys,
buzzards, and other fowl done in impossible
colors.

After that experience "our house" sim-
mered and shrivelled down from the Nor-
man-Gothic to plain, everyday, fin-de-siècle
architecture. We concluded that we could
get along with five rooms (although six
would be better), and we transferred our affections from that corner lot in the avenue
which had engaged our attention during the

decadent-renaissance phase of our enthusiasm to a modest point in Slocum's Addition, a locality originally known as Slocum's Slough, but now advertised and heralded by the press and rehabilitated in public opinion as Paradise Park. This pleasing mania lasted about two years. Then it was forever abated by the awful discovery that Paradise Park was the breeding spot of typhoid fever, and, furthermore, that old man Slocum's title to the property was defective in every essential particular.

Alice and I did not find it in our power either to overlook or to combat these trifling objections; with unabated optimism we cast our eyes elsewhere, and within a month we found another delectable biding place—this time some distance from the city—in fact, in one of the new and booming suburbs. Elmdale was then new to fame. I suppose they called it Elmdale because it had neither an elm nor a dale. It was fourteen miles from town, but its railroad transportation facilities were unique. The five-o'clock milk-train took passengers in to business every morning, and the eight-o'clock accommodation

5

brought them home again every evening; moreover, the noon freight stopped at Elmdale to take up passengers every other Wednesday, and it was the practice of every other train to whistle and to slack up in speed to thirty miles an hour while passing through this promising suburb.

I did not care particularly for Elmdale, but Alice took a mighty fancy to it. Our twin boys (Galileo and Herschel, named after the astronomers of blessed memory!) were now three years old, and Alice insisted that they required the pure air and the wholesome freedom of rural life. Galileo had, in fact. never quite been himself since he swallowed the pincushion.

We did not go to Elmdale at once; we never went there. Elmdale was simply another one of those curious phases in which our dream of a home abounded. With the Elmdale phase "our house" underwent another change. But this was natural enough. You see that in none of our other plans had we contemplated the possibility of a growing family. Now we had two uproarious boys, and their coming had naturally put us into pleasing doubt as to what similar emergencies might tran'spire in the future. So our five-room cottage had acquired (in our minds) two more rooms—seven altogether—and numerous little changes in the plans and decorations of "our house" had gradually been evolved.

As I now remember, it was about this time that Alice made up her mind that the reception-room should be treated in blue. Her birth had occurred in December, and therefore turquoise was her birth-stone and the blue thereof was her favorite color. I am not much of a believer in such things— in fact, I discredit all superstitions except such as involve black cats and the rabbit's foot, and these exceptions are wholly reasonable, for my family lived for many years in Salem, Mass. But I have always conceded that Alice has as good a right to her superstitions as I to mine. I bought her the prettiest turquoise ring I could afford, and I approved her determination to treat the reception-room in blue. I rather enjoyed the prospect of the luxury of a reception-room; it had ground the iron into my soul that,

7

ever since we married and settled down, Alice and I had been compelled in winter months to entertain our callers in the same room where we ate our meals. In summer this humiliation did not afflict us, for then we always sat of an evening on the front porch.

The blue room met with a curious fate. One Christmas our beneficent friend, Colonel Mullaly, presented Alice and me with a beautiful and valuable lamp. Alice went to Burley's the next week and priced one (not half as handsome) and was told that it cost sixty dollars. It was a tall, shapely lamp, with an alabaster and Italian marble pedestal cunningly polished; a magnificent yellow silk shade served as the crowning glory to this superb creation.

For a week, perhaps, Alice was abstracted; then she told me that she had been thinking it all over and had about made up her mind that when we got our new house she would have the reception-room treated in a delicate canary shade.

"But why abandon the blue, my dear?" I asked. "I think it would be so pretty to have the decoration of the room match your turquoise ring."

"That 's just like a man!" said Alice. "Reuben, dear, could you possibly imagine anything else so perfectly horrid as a yellow lampshade in a blue room?"

"You are right, sweetheart," said I. "That is something I had never thought of before. You are right; canary color it shall be, and when we have moved in I 'll buy you a dear little canary bird in a lovely gold cage, and we 'll hang it in the front window right over the lamp, so that everybody can see our treasures from the street and envy our happiness!"

"You dear, sweet boy!" cried Alice, and she reached up and pulled my head down and kissed her dear, sweet boy on his bald spot. Alice is an angel!

I fear I am wearying you with the prolixity of my narrative. So let me pass rapidly over the ten years that succeeded to the yellow-lamp epoch. Ten hard but sweet years! Years full of struggle and hopes, touched with bereavement and sorrow, but precious years, for troubles, like those we

have had, sanctify human lives. Children
came to us, and of these priceless treasures
we lost two. If I thought Alice would ever
see these lines I should not say to you now
that from the two great sorrows of those
years my heart has never been and never
shall be weaned. I would not have Alice
know this, for it would open afresh the
wounds her dear, tender mother-heart has
suffered.

Galileo and Herschel are strapping fellows. They have survived their juvenile ambi-
tions to be milkmen, policemen, lamp-light-
ers, butchers, grocerymen, etc., respectively.
Both are now in the manual-training school.
Fanny, Josephine and Erasmus—I have not
mentioned them before,—these are the children that are left to us of those that have
come in the later years. And, my! how
they are growing! What changes have
taken place in them and all about us! My
affairs have prospered; if it had n't been for
the depression that set in two years ago I
should have had one thousand dollars in
bank by this time. My salary has increased
steadily year by year; it has now reached a

sum that enables me to hope for speedy relief from those financial worries which en-
compass the head of a numerous household.
By the practice of rigid economy in family
expenses I have been able to accumulate a
large number of black-letter books and a fine
collection of curios, including some fifty
pieces of mediæval armor. We have lived
in rented houses all these years, but at no
time has Alice abandoned the hope and the
ambition of having a home of her own.
"Our house" has been the burthen of her
song from one year's end to the other. I
understand that this becomes a monomania
with a woman who lives in a rented house.

And, gracious! what changes has "our
house" undergone since first dear Alice pictured it as a possibility to me! It has passed
through every character, form, and style of
architecture conceivable. From five rooms
it has grown to fourteen. The reception
parlor, chameleon-like, has changed color
eight times. There have duly loomed up
bewildering visions of a library, a drawing-
room, a butler's pantry, a nursery, a laundry
—oh, it quite takes my breath away to re-

call and recount the possibilities which
Alice's hopes and fancies conjured up.

But, just two months ago to-day Alice
burst in upon me. I was in my study over
the kitchen figuring upon the probable date
of the conjunction of Venus and Saturn in
the year 1963.

"Reuben, dear," cried Alice, "I 've done
it! I 've bought a place!"

"Alice Fothergill Baker," says I, "what
do you mean!"

She was all out of breath—so transported
with delight was she that she could hardly
speak. Yet presently she found breath to
say: "You know the old Schmittheimer
place — the house that sets back from the
street and has lovely trees in the yard? You
remember how often we 've gone by there
and wished *we* had a home like it? Well,
I 've bought it! Do you understand, Reuben
dear? I 've bought it, and we 've got a
home at last!"

"Have you *paid* for it, darling ?" I asked.

"N-n-no, not yet," she answered, "but
I 'm going to, and you 're going to help me,
are n't you, Reuben?"

"Alice," says I, going to her and putting my arms about her, "I don't know what you 've done, but of course I 'll help you — yes, dearest, I 'll back you to the last breath of my life!"

Then she made me put on my boots and overcoat and hat and go with her to see her new purchase — "our house!"

II

OURSELVES AND OUR NEIGHBORS

EVERYBODY'S house is better made by his neighbors. This philosophical utterance occurs in one of those black-letter volumes which I purchased with the money left me by my Aunt Susan (of blessed memory!). Even if Alice and I had not fully made up our minds, after nineteen years of planning and figuring, what kind of a house we wanted, we could have referred the important matter to our neighbors in the confident assurance that these amiable folk were much more intimately acquainted with our needs and our desires than we ourselves were. The utter disinterestedness of a neighbor qualifies him to judge dispassionately of your requirements. When he tells you that you ought to do so and so or ought to have such and such a thing, his counsel should be heeded, because the probabilities are that he has made a careful study of you and he has unselfishly arrived at conclusions which intelligently contemplate your welfare. In planning for oneself one is too likely to be directed by narrow prejudices and selfish considerations.

Alice and I have always thought much of our neighbors. I suspect that my neighbors are my most salient weaknesses. I confess that I enjoy nothing else more than an informal call upon the Baylors, the Tiltmans, the Rushes, the Denslows and the other good people who constitute the best element in society in that part of the city where Alice and I and our interesting family have been living in rented quarters for the last six years. This informality of which I am so fond has often grieved and offended Alice. It is that gentle lady's opinion that a man at my time of life should have too much dignity to make a practice of "bolting into people's houses " (I quote her words exactly) when I know as well as I know anything that they are at dinner, and that a dessert in the shape of a rhubarb pie or a strawberry shortcake is about to be served.

There was a time when Alice overlooked this idiosyncrasy upon my part; that was before I achieved what Alice terms a national reputation by my discovery of a satellite to the star Gamma in the tail of the constellation Leo. Alice does not stop to consider that our neighbors have never read the royal octavo volume I wrote upon the subject of that discovery; Alice herself has never read that book. Alice simply knows that I wrote that book and paid a printer one thousand one hundred dollars to print it; this is sufficient to give me a high and broad status in her opinion, bless her loyal little heart!

But what do our neighbors know or care about that book? What, for that matter, do they know or care about the constellation Leo, to say nothing of its tail and the satellites to the stellar component parts thereof? I thank God that my hospitable neighbor, Mrs. Baylor, has never suffered a passion for astronomical research to lead her into a neglect of the noble art of compounding rhubarb pies, and I am equally grateful that no similar passion has stood in the way of good Mrs. Rush's enthusiastic and artistic construction of the most delicious shortcake ever put into the human mouth.

The Denslows, the Baylors, the Rushes, the Tiltmans and the rest have taken a great interest in us, and they have shared the enthusiam (I had almost said rapture) with which Alice and I discoursed of "the house" which we were going to have "sometime." They did not, however, agree with us, nor did they agree with one another, as to the kind of house this particular house of ours ought to be.   Each one had a house for sale, and each one insisted that his or her house was particularly suited to our requirements. The merits of each of these houses were eloquently paraded by the owners thereof, and the demerits were as eloquently pointed out by others who had houses of their own to sell "on easy terms and at long time."

It was not long, as you can well suppose, before Alice and I were intimately acquainted with all the weak points in our neighbors' residences.   We knew all about the Baylors' leaky roof, the Denslows' cracked plastering, the Tiltmans' back stairway, the Rushes' exposed water pipes, the Bollingers' defective chimney, the Dobells' rickety foundation. and a thousand other scandalous details which had been dinged into us and which we treasured up to serve as a warning to us when we came to have a house—"*the* house" which we had talked about so many years.

I can readily understand that there were those who regarded our talk and our planning simply as so much effervescence. We had harped upon the same old string so long—or at least Alice had—that, not unfrequently, even we smilingly asked ourselves whether it were likely that our day-dreaming would ever be realized. I dimly recall that upon several occasions I went so far as to indulge in amiable sarcasms upon Alice's exuberant mania. I do not remember just what these witticisms were, but I daresay they were bright enough, for I never yet have indulged in repartee without having bestowed much preliminary study and thought upon it.

I have mentioned our youngest son, Erasmus; he was born to us while we were members of Plymouth Church, and we gave him that name in consideration of the wishes of our beloved pastor, who was deeply learned in and a profound admirer of the philosophical works of Erasmus the original. Both Alice and I hoped that our son would incline to follow in the footsteps of the mighty genius whose name he bore. But from his very infancy he developed traits widely different from those of the stern philosopher whom we had set up before him as the paragon of human excellence. I have always suspected that little Erasmus inherited his frivolous disposition from his uncle (his mother's brother), Lemuel Fothergill, who at the early age of nineteen ran away from the farm in Maine to travel with a thrashing machine, and who subsequently achieved somewhat of a local reputation as a singer of comic songs in the Barnabee Concert Troupe on the Connecticut river circuit.

Erasmus' sense of humor is hampered by no sentiment of reverence. For the last five years he has caused his mother and me much

humiliation by his ribald treatment of the
subject that is nearest and dearest to our
hearts. In fact, we have come to be ashamed
of speaking of "the house" in Erasmus' hearing, for that would give the child a chance
to indulge in humor at the expense of a matter which he seems to regard as visionary as
the merest fairy tale. Now Galileo and Herschel are very different boys; they are making famous progress at the manual training
school. Galileo has already invented a churn
of exceptional merit, and Herschel is so deft
at carpentering that I have determined to let
him build the observatory which I am going
to have on the roof of the new house one
of these days. Galileo and Herschel are unusually proper, steady boys. And our daugh-
ters — ah! that reminds me.

Fanny is our oldest girl. She is going on
fifteen now. She favors the Bakers in appearance, but her character is more like her
mother's side of the family. If I do say it
myself, Fanny is a beautiful girl. If I could
have *my* way Fanny would be less given to
the social amenities of life, but the truth is
that the dear creature naturally loves gayety

and is bound to have it at all times and under all conditions. Her merry disposition makes her a favorite with all, and particularly with her schoolmates.

Now that I think of it, Willie Sears has been to see Fanny every evening for the last week. I wonder whether Alice has noticed it; I think I shall have to speak to her about it. Yet the probability is that Alice will resent the suggestion which my mention of the matter will convey. Alice has been saying all along that one particular reason why our new house should be a large one is that there would then be a room where Fanny could receive her company without being mortified almost to death by Erasmus' horrid intrusion and still more horrid remarks. At such times I forgive and adore Erasmus. It seems only yesterday that I bought her a bisque doll at the World's Fair, a bisque doll with pink eyes and blue hair, and now—oh, Fanny, are you no longer our little girl?

Still, we have Josephine, and I am sure she will honor us; for she was born six years ago under the conjunction of Jupiter and Venus, and while Mars was at perihelion.

Moreover, she is the seventh daughter of a seventh daughter, and there are those who believe that there is especial virtue in that. I named her after the French empress, not because I am a particular admirer of that remarkable but unfortunate woman's character, but for the reason that upon one occasion she secured a pension of eight hundred francs for the astronomer LeBanc, who had already added to the sum of human happiness by locating an asteroid near the left limb of the sun, and who subsequently discovered a greenish yellow spot on the outer ring of the planet Saturn. I never hear my dear little girl's voice or see her sweet face that I do not think of the planet Saturn; and never in the solemn stillness of night do I contemplate the scintillating glories of the ringed orb without being reminded of the fair, innocent babe asleep in her little white iron bedstead downstairs.

This sentimental association of objects widely separated in space has served to convince me that there is nothing, either in the heavens above or in the earth beneath, that has not its use, both profitable and pleasant.

III

WE MAKE OUR BARGAIN KNOWN

THE Schmittheimer place has occasioned Alice and me many heartburnings of envy the last three years. I recall that the first time we passed it Alice exclaimed: "There, Reuben, is just the place for us!" I agreed entirely with this proposition. The house stood back a goodly distance from the street upon a prominence that gave it an extended survey of the landscape, and afforded an exceptionally noble opportunity for an unobstructed view of the heavens upon cloudless nights. Alice particularly admired the lawn, for already she pictured to herself the pleasing sight of little Josephine and little Erasmus at play in the cool grass under the umbrageous trees.

And now, having yearned and pined for this particular abiding-place a many days, it

was really ours! Alice told me about it —
how she had comprehended the bargain (for
it was indeed a bargain!) — as we proceeded
together to inspect our new home. It seems
that that very morning, worn out with
waiting and inflamed by a determination to
do Now or to perish in the attempt, Alice had
sallied forth in quest of the precious game.
She had gone directly to the owner, had
subtly ingratiated herself in the confidence
of Mrs. Schmittheimer, and, in less than fifteen minutes' time, had made terms with
that amiable woman. And *such* terms! My
head fairly swims when I think of it.

Mrs. Schmittheimer is a widow. Since
her husband's demise two years ago come
next September, she has lived in compara-
tive solitude in the old home. She was not
wholly alone, for with characteristic Teutonic
thrift she had rented the lower part of the
house to a small family, consisting of a mechanic, his wife, their baby, and a small dog.
Mrs. Schmittheimer herself lived and moved
and had her being in the second story, doing
her own cooking and other housework, her
only companion being her faithful omnipres-

ent cat, the sex of which (I state this for a reason which will hereinafter transpire) was feminine. Although the good Mrs. Schmitt-heimer was not unfrequently visited by female compatriots who condoled with her and drank her coffee and ate her kuchen, after the fashion of sympathetic, suffering womanhood, she wearied of this loneliness; she was, in fact, as anxious to get away from the old place as Alice and I were to get into it.

So Alice and Mrs. Schmittheimer had little trouble in coming to an understanding mutually agreeable. The late Mr. Schmittheimer had always demanded the round sum of ten thousand dollars for the property under discussion, but the prevalence of hard times and the persuasive eloquence of my dear diplomatic Alice induced the late Mr. Schmittheimer's relict to consent to a reduction of the price to nine thousand five hundred dollars, "one thousand dollars in cash and the balance in five years at six per cent. interest, payable semi-annually."

"You see," said Alice to me, "that we practically get the place for five years by simply paying rent. We pay one thousand dollars down and fifty dollars a month interest. In five years there are sixty months. and in that time we shall have paid for this place four thousand dollars, which is but four hundred dollars more than we should have to pay if we remained in the house we are now living in at sixty dollars a month rental! You see, I have figured it all out, and figures can't lie!"

You will agree with me when I tell you right here that my wife Alice is a superior woman.

"Now we must be very careful," said Alice, "not to breathe a word about this to anybody until all the papers have been signed and the property has been transferred."

I suggested that in so serious a proceeding it might be wise to have the counsel of the more intimate of our neighbors; the Baylors, the Rushes and the Tiltmans had had experience in such matters. and might be of important service to us in this particular undertaking.

"No," said Alice. " we must guard against every possibility of failure. Our plan might leak out and reach the ears of the real-estate dealers, and then we should be hopelessly lost. Our neighbors mean well, but they are human. No, the only people I shall consult are the Denslows."

I saw at once the wisdom of this determination. The Denslows are most estimable folk and I admire and love them. Mrs. Denslow is of an exceptionally warm, generous, and liberal nature, while, upon the other hand, Mr. Denslow has the reputation of being the most cautious business man in our city; the consequence is that in the administration of affairs in the Denslow household you meet with that conservative happy medium which is beautiful to contemplate. Alice was right; our precious secret would be secure with the Denslows. In fact the Denslows would be of distinct help to us in the vast enterprise in which we had embarked. Mrs. Denslow would be prepared at all times to provide sympathy and enthusiasm, and Mr. Denslow would be constituted at once absolute engineer and watchdog of the business details of the affair.

But—I make the confession amid blushes

—I cannot prevaricate, neither can I dissemble. Alice knew the guilelessness and singleness of my nature, and she should not have imposed that dreadful oath of secrecy upon me. I would not for all the wealth of the Indies live over again the awful four hours which followed my solemn promise to Alice not to reveal the blissful tidings that we had bought the old Schmittheimer place! I felt as if I had committed a crime; I was as a haunted man must be. I dared not look my neighbors in the face lest they should read the sweet truth in my honest eyes.

Finally I broke completely down, for I could not stand it any longer. I actually believe that if I had kept silent another hour the dreadful consciousness of guilt would have swelled within me to such a bulk as to have burst me into fragments, which would now be travelling around aimlessly in space, like the lost Pleiad, or like the dismembered and stray tail of a comet. So I called my next neighbor, Rush, out behind his barn, and, under oath of secrecy, revealed the good news to him, and then I did likewise by neighbor Tiltman, and so on, in seemly progression, by all the other neighbors, until at last my confidence had been securely reposed in every one.

I cannot tell you what sweet relief I found in this proceeding. To my killing consciousness of guilt succeeded a peace which passeth all human understanding. There was a world of satisfaction, too, in being assured by each of those dear neighbors that we (Alice and I) had got the greatest bargain ever heard of, that we were the luckiest couple on earth, that the old Schmittheimer place was just exactly what we wanted, that the property would enhance double in value in less than a year, etc., etc., etc. Oh, it is good to have such neighbors as ours are!

The Denslows were quite as glad as the others were to hear of our bargain. Mrs. Denslow (bless her kind heart) began at once to picture the veritable paradise into which it were possible to transform the front lawn. In the exuberance of her fancy she portrayed winding gravel walks among rose bushes and beds of gay flowers; rustic bowers over which honeysuckle and ivy clambered; picturesque miniature Swiss cottages in the trees

for birds to nest in; an artificial lake well
stocked with goldfishes, and upon whose
tranquil bosom a swan or two would glide
majestically through the mist of the fountain
that perennially would shower down its
tinkling grace.

It was very pleasing to hear Mrs. Denslow
and Alice talk about these things with that
enthusiasm peculiar to their sex. Until "our
house" became a probability I did not really
know with what rapidity it were possible
for women-folk to discuss and to decide even
the most insignificant details of the subject
matter of their enthusiasm. As I recall, in
less than fifteen minutes' time after Alice had
confided our secret to Mrs. Denslow those
two amiable and superior women had it defi-
nitely settled what the color of the window
shades was to be and just how many brass-
headed tacks would be required to fasten
down the new Japanese rug with which it
was proposed to adorn the hardwood floor
of the library in the first story of "the addition" which had already been determined
upon. But Mrs. Denslow was no more pro-
lific of lovely suggestions than was Alice's

widowed sister Adah, who has made her home with us for the last two years. Adah's one o'ermastering ambition in life has been to build a house. In the autumn of 1881 she saw in a copy of "The National Architect" the picture and plans of a villa owned by a plutocrat at Narragansett Pier. She preserved this paper as sacredly as if it were one of the family archives, and upon the slightest pretext she brought it forth and exhibited it and dilated in extenso upon the surpassing advantages and beauties of the plutocratic villa.

When Adah learned that Alice and I had actually bought a place at last she fairly wept for joy, and she excitedly produced her creased and worn copy of "The National Architect" and besought us to remodel the old Schmittheimer "rookery" — that is what she dared to call it — into a villa! And when she was made to understand by means of numerous long and earnest representations that a villa could not even be dreamed of by poor folk, Adah was prepared to compromise the affair upon a basis involving our promise to build a colonial house like Maria's house in St. Jo.

This Maria, whose name is forever upon Adah's tongue, had been Adah's schoolmate back in St. Joseph, Missouri. Their friendship extended through the blissful years of their early wedded life. And at the present time they are as dear to each other as of yore. Adah presupposes that everybody else knows who Maria is, and so everybody is regaled perennially with Adah's loyal tributes to Maria's transcendent virtues. Occasionally Alice (who is without doubt the sweetest-natured creature in all the world) rebels against the example of Maria which Adah continually holds forth.

I have an instance just at hand. It could not have been more than half an hour ago that I heard Adah say: "Alice, do you know I've been thinking about it all the morning, and I don't see how you're going to get along without a closet in that little east room up-stairs."

"But," said Alice, "there seems to be no way of putting a closet into that room."

"Well, I think I've hit on a plan," said Adah, and she produced a Mme. Demorest pattern of a sleeve, upon which, with infinite pains, she had traced certain lines with the wreck of a pencil which little Josephine had tried to sharpen with the scissors.

"Yes, I see," said Alice, amiably; "but that would cut in upon the hall."

"Well, Maria had to do the same thing when she made her house over," said Adah, "and you 've no idea how nice it is."

"I don't care *what* Maria did," said Alice, bridling up. "This is *my* house, and I 'm not going to spoil a good hall by building any skimpy little closets! That room will do for Erasmus, and he does n't need any closet. So that is settled, once and forever!"

I heard all this, myself, from the next room. I did not interfere at all, for I make it a rule never to interpose in other people's disagreements. I will admit, however, that it rather wounded me to hear Alice call it "*my* house" instead of *our* house.

IV

THE FIRST PAYMENT

AS for Mr. Denslow, he agreed with other friends and neighbors that in our new old house we had secured a genuine bargain. But, as I have already indicated, Mr. Denslow was no day-dreamer; he had a way of viewing things that was severe in its practicality.

Now, I am in no sense a business man; you may already have suspected this truth. I am very far from being a fool, as those who have read my numerous treatises (particularly my " Essay to Prove the Probability of the Existence of an Atmosphere on the Other Side of the Moon ") will testify; but, having had little to do with the operations and methods of trade and commerce, I am not (I admit it freely) an expert in what in this great, bustling city of Chicago are termed affairs of the world.

Mr. Denslow, upon the other hand, is keenly in touch with these affairs; brought hourly during the day into contact and competition with scheming—and not always scrupulous—men, he has acquired an extensive knowledge of human nature of the rapacious type, and this knowledge has made him wary, alert, prudent, and reserved. It is perhaps this wide difference in our natures and our pursuits that has attracted Mr. Denslow and me to each other; at any rate our friendship has been profitable to both. Mr. Denslow's counsel upon several important occasions has been of vast value to me, and I flatter myself that upon one occasion at least I served Mr. Denslow to excellent purpose. This was two years ago, when, as perhaps you remember, my sun-spot theory was widely discussed by the newspaper press. I then told Mr. Denslow that the recurrence of the sun spots would surely induce a drought upon this planet, thereby causing a shortage in the crops; whereupon Mr. Denslow "cornered the wheat market" (as the saying is) and realized a handsome sum of money.

Alice has long recognized Mr. Denslow's merits as a man of business; she, too, has what, in lieu of a better term, our New England people call faculty. So it was natural that after having drunk deep (so to speak) at the fountain of Mrs. Denslow's enthusiasm, we should turn for serious advice and practical counsel to *Mr.* Denslow.

"This opportunity," said Mr. Denslow, "is one that comes only once in a lifetime. You must not let it escape you. We should go at once to Mrs. Schmittheimer and get her to sign an agreement to part with the property upon the terms specified. In order to bind the agreement we should pay her a small sum of money—oh, say one hundred dollars. The receipt, in the form of an agreement or contract signed by her, will bind the bargain in the contemplation of the law."

"But it is after dark already," said Alice. "Wouldn't it seem rather burglarious to make a descent upon the old lady at this hour?"

"And what is more to the point," said I, "the detail (trifling as it may appear) of planking down one hundred dollars is one which I happen just at this moment to be unprepared to provide for."

"The matter should be closed at once," said Mr. Denslow. "In a deal of this kind delay is too often disastrous. As for the one hundred dollars, I will lend you that amount, for a small cash payment is really necessary to bind the bargain."

My heart went out in gratitude to this noble gentleman. Never before had I felt more keenly the value of neighborly friendship.

"As this business is to be transacted in Mrs. Baker's name," said Mr. Denslow to me, "it would be better for you not to go with us to see Mrs. Schmittheimer. The presence of too many strangers might make the old lady shy of doing what we want her to do. See?"

Yes, I comprehended the intent of the suggestion, and I approved it. While it was far from my desire to take any advantage of the Widow Schmittheimer or of anybody else, I recognized the propriety of conserving our own interests to the extent of suffering no rights of our own to be either lost or jeoparded. So while Mr. Denslow and Alice went upon their business mission I remained with Mrs. Denslow and her interesting children and elucidated my theory of the ice-caps of the planet Mars. In less than an hour Mr. Denslow and Alice returned and exhibited with delight a receipt signed by Katherine Elizabeth Schmittheimer, which receipt, I was glad to see, was practically a contract to sell the property upon the terms specified in her original talk with Alice.

"The terms are certainly exceptionally advantageous!" said Mr. Denslow. "It will take some time — perhaps a week or ten days — to investigate the title; when this detail is satisfactorily disposed of you can pay down your one thousand dollars and take possession of the premises."

Pay down one thousand dollars? Ah, I had quite forgotten about *that*. In my enthusiasm over the prospect of a home of our own, and in the delirium induced by the delightful chatter about the paradise into which that front lawn and that old rookery (as Adah called it) were to be transformed, I had suffered all thought of the essential and inevitable first payment of one thousand dollars to slip quite out of my mind. Now this awful consideration, from which there could be no escape, took complete and exclusive possession of me. Where in the wide, wide world was I to get the one thousand dollars?

This was the question I put to Alice on the way home from the Denslows' that memorable evening. Alice knew as well as I did that my salary was sufficient only to cover the current expenses of the family. She knew as well as I did that the royalties from my books the last year were as follows:

" The Star Gamma in Leo and Its Satellite " . . . $1.00
" Mars and Its Ice-Caps " 75
" Probable Depth of the Bottle-Neck Seas as Indi-
    cated by the Spectroscope " 30
" Logarithms for the Nursery " 1.15
" Alphabetical Catalogue of Binary Stars " 05

    Total $4.45

Alice knew, too, as well as I did, that the whole amount of money I received from my lectures before the West Side Society for the Diffusion of Knowledge did not exceed seventy dollars last year. She knew all these things, and I told her so, and then I asked her where or how she fancied we were going to raise the one thousand dollars for the first payment on "our house." To my surprise, Alice was prepared—or at least she seemed to be prepared for this question.

"Reuben," said she, "I remember having heard Mr. Black say one day during his visit to us last summer that we ought to have a home, and that if we ever decided to buy one he would try his best to help us."

Now that Alice spoke of it I, too, recalled that friendly remark of Mr. Black's. A man who is drowning will catch at a straw. A man who has bought a house with nothing to pay for it is also predisposed to clutch. Our old friend Mr. Black now loomed up as my only sure salvation.

Mr. Black is upward of seventy years of age. He and my father went to school together in Maine, and subsequently they lived near each other in Cincinnati. Mr. Black had been a merchant; he had retired from

business rich. After my father's death, while
I was still a boy, this kind old friend was
good to me, taking an interest in my work
and my welfare. He had no children of his
own, and, if he did not regard me almost as
a son, I certainly grew to regard him almost
as a father. Mr. Black knew the value of
money and respected it. He gave freely, but
only where he was assured it was deserved
and would do actual good. A prudent, careful, economical man himself, he encouraged
prudence and thrift in others. He never
quite condoned what he regarded as extravagance upon my part in buying my fifty
pieces of mediæval armor, although it is to his
munificence that I am indebted for the six-
foot telescope with which I am wont to scan
the face of the heavens.

The upshot of talks with Alice and Adah
and the Denslows — to say nothing of other
neighbors with whom I confidentially consulted — the upshot of these talks was that
I determined to go to Cincinnati to confer
with Mr. Black upon the propriety of his ad-
vancing to me the money wherewith Alice
should make the first payment upon her—

I mean our house. To make short of a long story (for if there is one thing that I despise above all others it is prolixity), I went to Cincinnati and unfolded my business to my aged friend. Mr. Black appeared to be in no indecent haste to satiate my craving. He is not, and never was, a man of exuberant enthusiasms. I was rather pained when, upon learning of the unparalleled bargain we had secured in the Schmittheimer place, he did not go into raptures as did Mrs. Denslow, and Mrs. Baylor, and Mrs. Tiltman and the rest of our neighbors at home. So far from being carried away by any whirlwind of enthusiasm, Mr. Black maintained a placidity of demeanor amounting to stoicism; he plied me with questions about "titles," and "abstracts," and "indentures," and "mortgages," and "liens," and "incumbrances," and other things that I actually knew no more about than the veriest Bushman knows about the theory of Nebulæ.

To add to my embarrassment he solicited explicit information about the Schmittheimer place, in what subdivision it was located, and in what township. Had I been a veritable human encyclopædia I could hardly have satisfied that man's greed for information touching that particular spot. What knew I of tracts, of townships, of quarter sections or of subdivisions? Were I filled with a knowledge of these humdrum common- places, should I know aught of that enthusi- asm which thrills the being who, after many and long years of weary hoping and wait- ing, sees the object of his desires just within his grasp? Should Moses just in sight of the promised land be expected to give the dimensions of that delectable spot, and to locate it and bound it and map it off with the accuracy of a Rand & McNally town- ship guide?

I suppose that this conservatism is natural with some people — this lack of fervor, this absence of enthusiasm. Still I will admit Mr. Black's tranquillity — nay, his glacial com- posure — under the circumstances surprised and grieved me. I did not understand why the prospect and the promise of "our house" did not set Mr. Black — and, for that matter, all the rest of humanity — into the selfsame transports of delight which I experienced. Mind you, now, I am not complaining of nor am I finding fault with Mr. Black. I am simply chronicling happenings and observations. Mr. Black is a benevolent and beneficent man. He said to me at last: "Well, you can tell Alice that I will send her a draft for the money she needs, and within a fortnight I shall run up to take a look at your purchase."

I was in Cincinnati three days. I should have been there but two. A curious happening detained me. As I was going to the railway station from Mr. Black's house the evening of the second day I saw a man with a reflector telescope selling views of the moon at five cents apiece. The night was so auspicious for this diversion that I could not resist the temptation. Thus seduced, the time sped so quickly and the intoxication of the enjoyment was so complete that two hours slipped away before I awakened to a realization of my folly, which cost me somewhat over a dollar and a half, and compelled me to postpone my departure for home to the next day.

V

WE NEGOTIATE A MORTGAGE

ALICE and I supposed that as soon as we made that first payment upon the old Schmittheimer place we should take possession of it. We had hastened negotiations because naturally enough we were anxious to share the delights of the Eden which was to be ours. It transpired all too early in the proceedings, however, that the processes of the law are exceedingly exacting and provokingly tedious. With the one thousand dollars which Mr. Black gave us we fancied that we should be able to say to the widow Schmittheimer: "Here is your money; now let us move in."

It seems that the business is not done in that business-like way. As soon as the widow Schmittheimer contracted to part with her property at a stated price and upon stated

terms she awoke to a realization of the fact
that she ought to have the coöperation and
counsel of a lawyer — although for the life
of me I cannot see what there was left for a
lawyer to do. With a magnanimity and
generosity which bespoke the largeness of
his nature, Mr. Denslow volunteered his services as counsellor to the wary widow, and
I confess that I should have interposed no objection to having this versatile friend serve
in this capacity. But the widow chose to
decline the gratuitous services of Mr. Denslow, and to pay fifty dollars for the professional advice of a certain Lawyer Meisterbaum, not a bad fellow, but one of those
carping, superficial people who pretend to a
conscientiousness and a prudence and a zeal
which they actually do not possess.

After repeated meetings and the most annoying delays, Alice plainly told this Lawyer
Meisterbaum that he had more than earned
his fee by his puerile interferences with a
prompt and amicable adjustment of the affair.
Alice and Mr. Denslow and I agreed that,
if we had been left to ourselves, we could
have settled the business with the widow

Schmittheimer in half a day. However, I suppose that the lawyers must have a chance to make a living, and I can readily understand how a really conscientious lawyer might have the lingering remnant or suggestion of a desire to impress his client with the suspicion that he was earning his fee.

For fully a fortnight after my return from Cincinnati we were harassed by the delays of the law, or, more exactly speaking, by the exasperating crochets of the lawyer. Meanwhile there came letters of anxious inquiry from our munificent friend Mr. Black, for that estimable person, being aware of my predilection for ancient armor and other curios, found it difficult to disabuse his mind of the suspicion that his one thousand dollars might have been diverted from its original purpose, and misappropriated to what he esteemed the uses of folly. So it was with a feeling of great relief that finally I apprised our generous friend by telegraph that the transaction had been closed.

This end had not been reached, however, until Alice had put her signature and her seal to a curiously-phrased document which served (as I was told) as security to the widow Schmittheimer in case of "default in payment of interest or principal." This instrument is called, as I remember, a deed of trust, which seems to be another and a more polite name for a mortgage.

I protested against Alice's putting her signature to this document, which I still recognize as a covert foe to our happiness and prosperity. But Mr. Denslow assured us that the proceeding was wholly proper and businesslike, and Alice paid no heed to my expostulations. Never before had I had any experience in matters or with instruments of this kind, and I will admit that I have not even now any idea of what the purport of the document in question is, further than a distinct intuition that its involved syntax and complex and cloudy phraseology bode no good.

As soon as the transaction was closed the widow Schmittheimer burst into tears and loudly bewailed having parted with her home. I then learned that for the last ten days she had been almost constantly besieged by old friends of hers — the same who had been wont to consume her coffee and her kuchen and who now regaled her (in compensation, as it were, for her past hospitality) with reproachful assurances that she had been virtually swindled out of her beautiful property. The grief of this lonely and amiable woman touched me to the core, and I sought to assuage her melancholy by telling her that we should expect her to visit us, to which she replied amid tears and seeming gratitude that she would be sure to call every September and March, these being the months (as I afterward learned) in which the semi-annual interest, so called, fell due.

As you may suppose, while Alice and I, under the direction of Mr. Denslow, were worrying ourselves nearly to death over the miserable details of " closing " this transaction, our neighbors and Adah (Alice's sister) busied themselves with planning improvements in and for our new home. It was during this period that Adah met with one of those sorrows which benumb the sensitive feminine heart. In a moment of vandalism ever to be deprecated, little Erasmus discovered and took possession of that copy of "The National Architect" which contained the picture of the plutocratic villa at Narragansett Pier. This precious relic was put by the heedless boy to the base use of serving as a tail to a kite, and during one of the high winds the kite blew away, and there was an end to Adah's most precious possession! Thus perished the link that united Adah to the sweetest dream of her maturer years.

However, this mishap did not wholly abate Adah's interest in our affairs. In answer to Adah's solicitation a long letter had come from Maria, bearing the blissful promise that a carefully made plan of Maria's house of St. Joe (drawn by Maria herself upon a fly leaf excerpted from Maria's favorite volume, "The Life of Mary Lyon") would soon be forwarded for our enlightenment and delectation. Maria felt kindly toward us, and her sympathies had been awakened to their very depths by a tender souvenir Adah had sent her — a leaf plucked from one of the lilac bushes on the old Schmittheimer place. Both Adah and Maria belong to that old-school class of proper feminine folk who never pick but always pluck flowers.

Well, Adah and the neighbors kept as busy as a bee in a bottle planning changes that they deemed necessary in our house. When we got through with that dilly-dallying, shilly-shallying Lawyer Meisterbaum, Alice and I found out that Adah and the neighbors had left little for us to do except to approve their plans and pay for the execution thereof.

There had been a kind of tacit understanding all along that such changes as we made in the Schmittheimer house should be superintended by an architect-carpenter who was cordially recommended by Mrs. Denslow. This important person's name was Silas Plum, and he had a shop in Osgood Avenue, opposite one of our most fashionable and most prosperous cemeteries. Mrs. Denslow always called him Uncle Si, and this circumstance rather prejudiced me in favor of him. The facts, too, that Uncle Si was not overcrowded with business, that he was considerate in his charges, and that he was of so great versatility that he could

boss the plumbing as well as the carpentering—these facts confirmed us in the opinion
that Uncle Si was just the man for our needs.

I went with Mrs. Denslow to call upon
this gifted and honest son of toil. His modest place of business was indicated to the
passer-by by this insinuating sign:

SILAS PLUM, CARPENTER & BUILDER.
☞ COFFIN BOXES A SPECIALITY.

I am not a superstitious person. I think
I have already told you so. Still I have instincts and intuitions; and you, who are not
wholly dead to the subtle influences of the
more delicate sentiments, will probably sympathize with me when I admit that Mr.
Plum's sign did not inspire me with that
enthusiasm which is at least comforting to
the possessor. The reference to Mr. Plum's
"speciality" was what cast a temporary
gloom over me, but Mrs. Denslow was not
one of those who suffer a detail so insignifi-

cant as this to stand in her way; so I was bounced into Uncle Si's shop and presented to Uncle Si in propria persona.

Uncle Si impressed me as being a very trustworthy man. He looked not unlike myself; his gaunt, sinewy frame betokened severe practicability, and his calm blue eyes and large straight mouth combined to give his face an unmistakable and convincing expression of candor. Of speech he was monosyllabic, and this peculiarity pleased me, for I have always admired and always cultivated directness and terseness, there being nothing else more distasteful to me than the prolixity, diffuseness, pleonasm, amplification, redundance, and copia verborum of some people. I told Uncle Si all about the new purchase we had made, and I drew upon a pine board a fairly correct plan of the Schmittheimer house as it now stood. I gave him to understand that numerous and important changes were required, and that I desired to secure from him an estimate as to the cost of those changes.

"I can't tell how much it will be till I know what you want," said Uncle Si.

I recognized the justness of this remark, yet at the same time I felt bitter toward Uncle Si for not knowing without being told. To tell the truth, *I* didn't know. I had heard Alice and Adah talking in a general way about "closets" and a "new hall," and "hardwood floors" and — and — and things of that kind; I remembered having heard some discussion of a prospective "addition," and — yes — I now recalled that the front porch would have to be rebuilt. Hoping to conceal my utter ignorance, I told Uncle Si that we wanted "lots of changes," but this would not satisfy the exasperating man; he insisted upon particulars, upon "specifications," as he termed them.

Of course I was unable to give them; so was Mrs. Denslow. The only really distinct idea Mrs. Denslow had of the transformation contemplated by Alice was one concerning the front lawn, and involving gravel walks between flower beds and under umbrageous trees; exotics perennially in bloom; Swiss tree boxes, from which the lark carolled by day and the nightingale warbled at night; an artificial lake, in which goldfishes swam and

upon whose translucent bosom majestic
swans glided gracefully — I assure you that
Mrs. Denslow has the soul of a poet!

But these delightful fancies did not interest
Uncle Si, because they did not concern him
or his trade. So we compromised the matter by appointing an hour that evening for
Uncle Si to call and talk it all over with Alice.
This was, seemingly, the only way out of
the dilemma. All I knew was what I didn't
want, or, rather, what *we* didn't want. Our
many and long and earnest conversations
with the neighbors had determined numerous
important points. We didn't want a roof
like the Baylors' roof; nor water-pipes like
the Rushes'; nor backstairs like the Tiltmans'; nor plastering like the Denslows';
nor dormer-windows like the Carters'; nor
a kitchen sink like the Plunkers'; nor smoky
chimneys like the Bollingers'; nor a skimpy
little conservatory like the Mayhews'— in
fact, there were so many things we *didn't*
want that it seemed to me that if Uncle
Si had been moderately ingenious or had
given his imagination full rein, he might
have guessed what we *did* want. and so

have gone ahead without fear of incurring
our displeasure.

It was perhaps better, however, that, before undertaking his task, Uncle Si should
require some hint or intimation of what
would be expected of him. I am the last
man in the world to discourage what is ordinarily regarded and accepted as reasonable
precaution against embarrassment and adversity.

VI

I AM BESOUGHT TO BUY THINGS

ALICE had her talk with Uncle Si and issued therefrom with the conviction that Uncle Si was a paragon of integrity and carpentering skill. As for Uncle Si, he must have gathered together a pretty fair general idea of what Alice wanted, for he promised to return the next day with plans and details and with an estimate of what the contemplated improvements would cost.

Meanwhile another complication had arisen. The people to whom the widow Schmittheimer had rented the lower part of the house declined to vacate the premises unless we paid them a bonus of fifteen dollars. Alice indignantly protested that we had no fifteen dollars to throw away, and I recognized the truth of this proposition. Still, a visit to the recalcitrant tenants convinced me that they were poor folk and could ill afford to bear the expense of moving. Another circumstance that made me feel rather kindly toward these people was that their name was Mitchell, and, although they made no such claim, it pleased me to fancy that they were of kin to that distinguished family which has contributed so largely to the glory of native astronomical research.

Actuated, therefore, by the most honorable impulses, I gave these people fifteen dollars which I borrowed for that purpose from my most estimable neighbor, Mrs. Tiltman, upon the understanding that I should pay it back when I heard from ''The Sidereal Torch,'' to which publication I had sent a carefully prepared essay on Encke's comet. In this wise a matter which might have caused us much delay and vexation was quickly and amicably disposed of. I did not tell Alice of what I had done, for although Alice is (as I have already assured you) the most amiable of her sex, she cannot brook what she regards as an imposition, and this inclination to resent seeming overbearance in others has not unfrequently put us to expense and involved us in embarrassment.

Another episode which is still fresh in my memory I cannot forbear relating. Alice came to me one day not long ago— it was perhaps three weeks since — and insisted that I should attend to having the correct name of the avenue in which we were to live put upon the lamp-posts at the corners of that avenue. I could not guess what Alice meant until she informed me that, although the name of that thoroughfare had by ordinance of the City Council been changed from Mush Street to Clarendon Avenue, the old name of Mush Street had (by a singular inadvertence) been suffered to remain upon the lamp-posts along that highway.

"The idea!" cried Alice, indignantly. "Do you suppose I would live upon Mush Street? Do you suppose I ever would have bought that house and lot if I had suspected even for a moment that they were not in Clarendon Avenue? Mush Street is just horrid — everybody else thinks so, and I know it! I won't have it Mush Street; it's Clarendon Avenue, and I'm going to have

Clarendon Avenue engraved on my cards! Reuben, you must see at once that the lamp-posts are changed."

I confess that so far as I myself am concerned it matters not whether my abiding place be in Mush Street or in Clarendon Avenue so long as I am comfortably bedded and fed and my family are well provided for. Names are, at best, arbitrary things. Moreover, I was well aware (and you will see for yourself if you consult a map of our city) that that thoroughfare which has been re-named Clarendon Avenue is actually Mush Street, or, at any rate, a continuation of Mush Street. However, I had a regard for that sense of feminine pride which made Alice revolt against Mush Street. I am aware that the conspicuous characteristics of Mush Street for many miles are goats and fortune-tellers and coal yards and rumshops and mid-wiveries; these glaring features are by no means such as the élite of our society care to affect. Conceding that my indifference to these idiosyncrasies should not be suffered to stand in the way of the natural current of Alice's womanly pride, I promised to do

my best toward effecting what Alice required, and I am now engaged upon a me-
morial to the Mayor and the Board of Alder-
men praying that the lamp-posts in Clarendon
Avenue be purged of that lettering which
suggests the commonplace antecedents of
that thoroughfare.

I find that Alice is not alone in her wretch-
edness. It appears that our friends Lawyer
Miles and Mr. Redleigh and their families
are at present engaged in the momentous
task of getting the name of the street in
which they live changed from Cemetery
Avenue to Sportland Place. And our other
friends two blocks west of us are greatly
agitated just now because the name of their
aristocratic thoroughfare has, by a whim of
the municipal authorities, been changed from
Alexander Avenue to Osgood Street. I have
mentioned these facts to Alice, but no sense
of that sympathy which is said to arise from
the companionship of misery seems to recon-
cile my dear wife to the plebeian association
which the mere mention of Mush Street
suggests.

The Sunday morning after we had actually bought the Schmittheimer place the city newspapers made a record of the event in their "society column," and added that it was "understood that in their beautiful new home Prof. and Mrs. Baker would entertain lavishly." I was inclined to take exception to this item, which I regarded as a vulgar parade of our private affairs; moreover, the innuendo was wholly untruthful. Alice and I did not intend to "entertain" at all; we could not afford to "entertain." What would Mr. Black say if by chance he were to get hold of a copy of any of those Sunday morning newspapers and read that mendacious paragraph? He would not only lament the one thousand dollars which he had just advanced; worse than that, he would forever shut down on those other acts of similar generosity which, I am free to say, Alice and I counted among the pleasing probabilities of the near future.

I repeat that this untruthful notoriety through the medium of the "society column" displeased me, and I am sure I should have spoken my mind very freely about it if I had not heard Alice reading the item with

evident gusto to her sister Adah. My amazement was increased when Alice asked me to
secure a dozen extra papers for her, as she
wished to send marked copies to certain
fashionable society acquaintances and to several of her relatives in Maine! I can picture
the rural astonishment with which Cousin
Jabez Fothergill of Biddeford Pool and the
Strattons of North Moosehead will read of
our good fortune. I more than half suspect
that in a moment of triumphant revenge and
in a spirit of cruel malice Alice sent a copy
of the paper to Miss Mears at Pocatapaug.
Miss Mears is little to me now, but once I
called her Hepsival, and even after these
many years of separation I would fain undo
any act of spite which her successful rival,
Alice, might attempt.

The Monday following the publication of
this strangely malevolent item was an unusually busy day with me. I seemed suddenly to have become the target of every
man who had anything to sell. I was waited
upon by fruit-tree venders, lightning-rod
agents, fire underwriters, plumbers, gas-
fitters, painters, and an innumerable army of

persons having horses, cows, pigs, chickens, shade trees, patent hitching posts, smoke-consumers, Pasteur filters, shrubbery, lawn statuary, fancy poultry, garden utensils, and patent paving to dispose of. I really cannot realize how I got rid of them all, for a more affable and persuasive lot of gentlemen I never before had met with. Come to think of it, I have *not* got rid of them. They continue to cultivate my acquaintance and on account of their attentions (polite but persistent) I have been compelled to lay aside temporarily my investigation into the character of the atmosphere around Aldebaran, a most delicate work upon which I am hoping to rear the superstructure of my fame.

I admit that these attentions rather flatter me; it is possible that after a time — say a year or two — I may weary of the courteous gentleman who is now seeking to sell me a dozen apple-trees, one-third cash, balance in ten years. I may, in the lapse of time, become indifferent to the blandishments of him who daily for the last two months has been trying to convince me that I cannot reach the summum bonum of human happi-

ness until I have invested four dollars in
Perkins' patent automatic garden rake and
step-ladder combination. The gentleman
who has the smoke-consumer, the gentleman who deals in shrubbery, the gentleman
who advocates lightning rods, and the other
gentlemen who represent the tantamount
interests of lawn statuary, fancy poultry,
patent paving, etc., etc., etc.—I may, in the
flight of years, become insensible to their
charms, for there is no change that is not
rendered possible by the capricious offices
of Time. But at present I can hardly realize
how these people can ever be other than
they now are — near to me, as I know, and
dear to me, as I feel.

I did not suspect, before I became a householder, that the mere possession of property
was capable of making a man an object of
such unflagging interest to his fellow creatures. I find it very pleasing — the solicitude
with which these newly-made acquaintances
(the venders, agents, and other polite gentlemen) regard me, and attend upon me,
and seek to gain my approval. It is sweet
to be beloved.

In the very height of this enjoyment, however, there are considerations which serve to cause me feelings of disquietude. My conscience constantly reproves me for the deception which I am practising upon these people. It occurred to me several weeks ago that I had no right to pose as the proprietor of our new house. The new house and its circumadjacent real estate belong not to me, but to Alice and to her heirs and assigns forever. I have no proprietary rights in that house or upon that expansive lawn: If I am there, it is simply as a piece of furniture, like the stove, or the clock, or the centre-table. I am simply tolerated, perhaps as an object of ornament, perhaps as an object of use. This is a humiliating confession: the thought that it is actually true pains me poignantly.

I never supposed I was a moral coward, but I must be: otherwise I would weeks ago have called an open-air mass-meeting of the apple-tree agents, the fire-underwriters, the patent pavers and the others, and confessed to them that their attentions were misdirected, and that I was not in fact *the* fortunate being whose lot they sought to better.

A strangely craven consideration withheld me from this manly course. I suspected that as soon as I divulged the truth I would be forsaken by this troupe — this retinue of unctuous courtiers. In my imaginings I beheld myself deserted and alone, while the vast army of my quondam attendants and flatterers tagged after and surrounded and fawned upon Alice, the real purchaser and actual owner of our new place!

I make a candid exposition of these things, not more for the purpose of relieving my conscience of its long pent-up misery than for the purpose of disclosing that which may happily serve as a warning to my fellow-beings. I long ago discovered that one of the compensations of human folly is the example which that folly affords for the discreet guidance of others.

VII

OUR PLANS FOR IMPROVEMENTS

THE result of the numerous conferences between Alice and Uncle Si was rather surprising to me. It involved the expenditure of somewhat more than three thousand dollars. However, a letter had been received from our beneficent friend, Mr. Black, in which that estimable gentleman expressed the conviction that we ought not to try to live in a house that did not have the ordinary conveniences of a modern city home, and that we should add whatever improvements we deemed necessary to our comfort; these pleasing expressions of opinion were supplemented by the still more pleasing intimation that Mr. Black would advance us whatever sum was necessary to the provision of the changes and innovations we deemed expedient. It was evident that Mr.

Black was most kindly disposed toward us; at the same time our munificent patron took occasion to caution us against extravagance and to impress upon us a sense of the necessity of constant and rigorous economy — "especially and particularly in the direction of those vanities which simply gratify an individual whim, and are of no practical value whatsoever."

Alice read this last sentence aloud to me several times, for it expressed exactly her opinion of my fondness for mediæval armor. I am making no complaint of the sly satisfaction which Alice seemingly takes in twitting me with my weakness. I expect to have a glorious revenge by and by when we move into our new house, and when Alice discovers how very appropriate and ornamental my mediæval armor will be, set up against the walls and in the corners of the front hall.

Fortified by the letter from Mr. Black, we had little difficulty in planning the most charming improvements. I make use of the plural personal pronoun, although if I were testifying upon oath I should feel compelled

to admit that I myself had precious little to
do with the planning. It grieved me considerably to observe that while the neighbors generally, and Mrs. Denslow particularly, were diligently consulted as to every
detail of the new house, an expression of
my wishes, views, and advice was not only
not solicited, but, when volunteered, seemed
to be regarded as an impertinence. It occurred to me at such times that prosperity
by no means improved Alice's temper, but
I should perhaps have taken into consideration the circumstance that this particular
period was one of exceptional excitement,
and that had the same sense of responsibility
which burdened Alice been put upon me, I,
too, should have exhibited an irritability
wholly foreign to my nature under normal
conditions and environments.

It was determined to reconstruct certain
parts of the old Schmittheimer residence and
to build an addition of two stories, the first-
floor room to be devoted to the purposes of
a library or living room, and the room in
the second story to be Alice's bed-chamber.
A vast number of closets were contemplated,

for, as you are presumably aware, woman-
kind are passionately fond of closets, and
happy, thrice happy, is the husband who is
accorded the inestimable boon of suspend-
ing his Sunday suit from a nail therein. As
for myself, I have always regarded the average closet as an ingenious device of the evil
one for the propagation and encouragement
of moths.

Among other contemplated innovations
were a butler's pantry and a conservatory.
I approved of the latter, but not of the
former. I foresaw in that butler's pantry a
pretext, if not a reason, for the purchase of
china, crockery, and glassware, to be used
only when we had company and to be hid-
den away at other times until broken by
careless servants.

A conservatory had for years been one
of my most pleasing desires. Although I
know little of them, I am fond of flowers,
particularly of those which others care for
and which do not breed or abound in creep-
ing things. But the use to which I was
ambitious to put my—or our—conservatory was that of an aviary. I love all pet

birds, and one of my sweetest day dreams has been that which possessed me of a large glass room or bower well stocked with canaries, linnets, bullfinches, robins, wrens, Java sparrows, love birds, and paroquets. I have often pictured to myself the delight I should experience in entering into this heaven of song and in caressing these feathered pets, in feeding them and in teaching them pretty tricks and games. I recall those pleasant boyhood days when a pet crow, and a flock of pigeons, and two baby hawks afforded me rapture and solicitude combined. Then followed an experience with a matronly hen and her brood of chicks.

I am not ashamed to say that I loved these friends of my youth and that I still reverence their memories. Nor am I ashamed to tell you that for several years after I reached maturity a particular object of my affections was a wee canary bird that sang sweet songs to me and played daintily with my finger whenever I thrust it into the little rascal's cage. Alice insists that I actually cried when that silly little creature died; may be I did, for I am a very, very foolish fellow.

One of the things I have never been able
to understand is why Alice, with all her gen-
tleness and tenderness, has so violent an
antipathy to bird and brute pets. Alice actually seems to dislike birds and dogs with
the same zeal with which I love them. At
times — you will hardly believe it — Alice
has exhibited Neronian cruelty and hardness
of heart. I remember that on one occasion
she caught a harmless, innocent little blue
mouse in the pantry. She fully intended to
drown the helpless creature — as if this world
were not big enough for mice and men to
live and be happy in! I had great difficulty
in rescuing the tiny rodent from his captor,
and I remember the satisfaction I had in
giving him his liberty under the kitchen
porch of neighbor Rush's house next
door.

At first Alice was kindly disposed toward
the conservatory scheme, but in an unguarded moment one day I chanced to breathe
a suggestion that a combination conserva-
tory-bird cage would do very nicely, and
that settled the fate of my pleasant dreamings
forever.

73

But I seldom argue these things with Alice. The conservatory is now a shattered dream, and the butler's pantry is inevitable. The graceful alcove, which was to have been the conservatory (with aviary features), is to be provided with a permanent, stationary seat which Adah is to upholster in a pattern which Maria has promised to send from St. Joe. Whenever I think of it there rise up before my mind's eye visions of stolen meetings in that alcove, and whispered interviews, in which I fancy I see our daughter Fanny figuring as an active participant, and then I devoutly pray that little Erasmus' vigilance may be increased a thousand-fold.

I was informed in good time that the library was to be virtually the living-room for the family. It was here that casual callers were to be received and entertained; here the errand boys who delivered packages from the downtown shops were to leave their goods and get their receipts; here the laundryman was to wait every Monday morning while Adah gathered up my hebdomadal bundle of linen for the wash; here

were the children to gather for a frolic every
evening after the humble vesper meal.

I am wondering whether Alice and Adah
and the neighbors will approve of my dearly
cherished plan to have one of the tall clocks
stationed in one corner, and my very old
Suffolk oak table in another corner, and in
still another the curious old sofa which Aunt
'Gusty has promised to send me from Darien,
Georgia. I am painfully aware that Alice
and Adah and the neighbors regard the
beautiful furniture in which I delight as
"old trumpery."

When we first looked at the Schmittheimer place Alice exclaimed, upon being
ushered into one of the rooms: "Now this
is just the room for Reuben and his old trumpery!" It is twenty-two feet long and eighteen feet wide, and there are windows to the
north, west, and south. Curiously enough,
the chimney runs up through the middle of
this room, presenting an appearance at once
novel and grotesque. Alice assures me that
this will prove a unique and charming feature, for she intends to put innumerable
shelves around the chimney, and place

thereon the interesting and valuable curios, the purchase of which has kept me involved in financial embarrassment for the last twenty years.

Alice has settled it in her own mind just where in my new room each bit of my beloved furniture shall be located — the mahogany chest of drawers, the old secretary, the four-post bedstead, the haircloth trunk, the oak book-case, the corn-husk rocker, the cuckoo clock, the Dutch cabinet — yes, each blessed piece has already had its place assigned to it, even to the old red cricket which Miss Anna Rice sent me from her Connecticut home twelve years ago. I am indeed the most fortunate of men; for who but my Alice *could* be so sweet and self-abnegatory as to take upon her own dear little shoulders the burden of responsibilities that elsewise would weigh upon her husband?

VIII

THE VANDALS BEGIN THEIR WORK

AT the regular April meeting of the Lake Shore Society of Antiquarians I met my old and valued friend, Belville Rock, and told him of the important venture which Alice had made. He seemed greatly pleased at the prospect of our having a home of our own, and after making careful inquiries into the extent and character of the improvements we contemplated he bade me tell Alice that he wanted to pay the bill for the painting of the exterior of the house. "I desire to do somewhat toward beautifying your premises," said he, "and I don't know that I can do better than to paint the house. You understand, of course, that my long and intimate acquaintance with you and Alice warrants me in proposing as a friendly act what elsewise might be regarded as an impertinence."

I hastened to assure Mr. Rock that both Alice and I knew him to be utterly incapable of any word or deed that could by any means be misconstrued into an impertinence. We had known this amiable gentleman for the period of twenty years. It was he who proposed me for membership of the Lake Shore Society of Antiquarians, and it was he who provided the means wherewith I published my first book, entitled "A Critical View of the Causes of Eclamptic and Traumatic Idiocy."

This was at the time in my career when I supposed I had good reason to believe that all human mental and physical ills are directly traceable to the influence of the moon, which theory was suggested to me by the discovery that cabbages thrive when planted in the first quarter of the moon and invariably pine when planted in the full of the moon. I am still more or less of a believer in this theory, and it is my purpose to renew my investigations and experiments in this direction, particularly so far as cabbages are involved, for I mean to have a kitchen garden (with Alice's permission) as soon as we

move into our new place in Mush Street —
pardon me, I mean Clarendon Avenue.

Belville Rock has always exhibited a
friendly interest in me and my welfare. He
is president of a savings bank and is concerned in numerous mercantile and spec-
ulative enterprises. He belongs to many
clubs and social organizations, and is president of the Sons of Vermont, the Sons of
New York, the Sons of Rhode Island, the
Sons of Michigan, and the other Sons who
have effected formal organizations in this city.
He is treasurer of most of the current enterprises and he is recognized as a leader of
distinct influence in the several political parties which control public affairs locally.

Mr. Rock commands the happy faculty of
divorcing himself wholly from business during those hours which he has dedicated to
sociability. He declines to discuss monetary
matters outside his room at the bank. I recall
how, upon several occasions when I have
approached him upon the delicate subject of
negotiating a trifling temporary loan, he has
dismissed the matter by reminding me that
he had·certain days which he set apart for

business of this character, and that at other times he devoted himself exclusively to the consideration of other things.

I recall, too, that after persistent inquiry (having, possibly, selfish ends in view), I learned from Cashier Bolton, who is Mr. Rock's marble-hearted alter ego, that Mr. Rock's hours for the consideration of all applications for personal accommodations were from 7.55 to 8 a.m., every other Thursday. This may strike the average person as a unique singularity, but I find it easy to understand how a man so numerously interested in affairs as Mr. Rock is should find it imperative to regulate his business and social conduct with the most methodical and most exacting system.

You can depend upon it that I lost no time in apprising Alice and Adah and our neighbors of Mr. Rock's munificent proposition, and I hardly need assure you that by all Mr. Rock's generosity was warmly applauded. The incident gave rise to a new phase in the sequence of events, for immediately a discussion arose as to the color which we ought to paint our new house, and this discussion continued with increasing vigor for several days. Adah was characteristically earnest in her advocacy of a soft cream yellow, that being the shade adopted by Maria when she repainted her St. Joe domicile — a soft cream yellow, with the blinds in a delicate brown, that was Adah's choice as inspired by her memory of Maria's habitation. The Baylors suggested a poetic grayish tint, which they insisted would look specially pretty through the foliage of the fine old trees in the front yard. The Tiltmans preferred a light brown, and the Rushes a bright yellow. As for Mrs. Denslow, she raised her voice in favor of "white, with green blinds," for, as she wisely argued, it was not possible to find a more appropriate combination for a house that had been a farmhouse and that would retain (even after we had rehabilitated it) the most salient characteristics of a farmhouse.

Alice and I agreed with Mrs. Denslow (as we generally do), and our determination was confirmed when we subsequently learned, upon inquiry of Mr. Krome, the painter, that white paint was as expensive a paint as could be selected. It was our desire, in our choice of paint, to do nothing likely to lessen or to detract from the lustre of the princeliness of Mr. Rock's liberality. Mr. Rock had set no limitations to his munificence; far be it from us to do that which might be construed wrongfully as inappreciation of that munificence. It was the part of friendship to premise that Mr. Rock's intentions were large, and then it behooved us to see that those intentions were carried out upon a scale of equal scope. We decided, therefore, that the paint should be white, and that it should be carriage paint.

Uncle Si had advised us to have plenty of light and air admitted to " the addition " by means of numerous windows. According to the rude plan he submitted for Alice's approval. " the addition " when completed would have looked like a collection of windows of every size and shape. This was before Mr. Rock offered to paint the house. After Mr. Rock's proposal was made to and accepted by us it occurred to us that it would result in a considerable saving to us if we were to limit the number of windows and devote the space (thus economized) to clapboarding. This would involve a larger expense upon Mr. Rock's part, but it could not be denied that Mr. Rock could better afford paying for paint than we could afford paying for window frames and glass.

I think it likely that I should have called on Mr. Rock to learn his preference in the matter had the "every other Thursday" been nearer at hand. But Mr. Krome, the painter, and Uncle Si, the boss carpenter, required a speedy decision, and so we went ahead without consulting our munificent friend. Mr. Krome thereupon volunteered to do our painting by the square yard, instead of by the square foot (as is the customary proceeding); he admitted, with a candor rarely met with in his profession, he could as well afford to do our house in white carriage paint by the square yard as other rival painters could afford to do it in common white lead by the square foot. I assured Mr. Krome of my determination to spare no pains to coöperate with him in every honest and ambitious endeavor at Mr. Rock's expense.

So now, the widow Schmittheimer having vacated the premises, the work of rehabilitation began in earnest. Men with wheelbarrows and spades and picks made their appearance and started in to demolish walls and to excavate sand at a marvelous rate. Presently a cavernous space yawned where it was proposed to locate the cellar where the steam-heating apparatus was to stand. The sand taken from this spot was barrowed out and dumped in a pile over the horseradish bed in the back yard.

This was the first piece of vandalism I noticed, and I protested against it. Not long thereafter I discovered that the workmen engaged at battering down the partitions in the upper part of the house were piling up the refuse scantling and laths on the currant and gooseberry bushes in the side yard. I protested again, and so I kept on protesting, for hardly a day passed that I did not detect the workmen about that house at some piece of lawlessness jeoparding the cherry trees, or the lilac bushes, or the tulips, or the roses, or the peonies, or the asparagus bed.

Cui bono—to what good ? With as much

effect might the wild man of Borneo rail at Capella because her silvery, twinkling light is seventy-one years in reaching this distant planet.

I am unalterably opposed to the wanton destruction of life. Moreover, it seems to me that the trees, the shrubbery, the vines and the flowers on the Schmittheimer place have certain rights which the invaders ought to respect. At any rate, I spent the better part of two days transplanting a number of the currant and gooseberry bushes, and although I had a stiff neck and a very lame back for a considerable time thereafter I felt more than compensated therefor by the conviction that I had saved the lives of friends who would duly give me practical proof of their gratitude.

There were certain acts of lawlessness that I could neither prevent nor repair. One grieved me particularly. The plumber hitched his horse to a tree in the front yard one morning, and, before the damage he had done was discovered, the herbivorous beast had eaten up a white lilac bush and a snowball bush, thus completing a destruc-

'tion for which there would seem to be no compensation. Up(another occasion a stray cow invaded the premises and laid waste the tulip bed and chewed off the tender buds on the choicest of the rose bushes.

But the most extensive and the most hideous depredations were committed by human beings under pretext of necessity and of interest in my behalf. I refer now to those remorseless men who came first and tore up the beautiful lawn and cut away the roots of trees and digged a deep, long pit in which to lay sewer pipes; who came again and committed another similar atrocity under plea of laying a water-pipe; who came still again and for the third time abused and seared and seamed and blighted that lawn for the alleged purpose of laying a gas-pipe! O civilization! what crimes are committed in thy name!

These experiences sobered and saddened me to a degree that was strangely new to me. At times I felt embittered against all the world. But as there is no cloud that has not its silver lining, so there were pleasant little happenings which ever and anon seemed to relieve my despondency. On one occasion Uncle Si said to me cheerily: "We 're going to have good luck from this time on." "What do you mean?" I asked. "Come along with me and see for yourself," said he.

Uncle Si led the way into the house and down into the basement. He pointed to an old valise that, spread open, lay under the stairs amid the débris which the masons had left.

"That 's what I mean," said Uncle Si, "and it brings good luck every time!"

I saw that the old and abandoned valise contained a tabby cat at whose generous dugs six wee kittens were tugging industriously. The widow Schmittheimer had left her home and gone elsewhere, but faithful tabby remained behind, true to that instinct which makes the feline unalterably loyal to locality.

I never before liked cats; I have always positively disliked them because they kill birds. Yet, do you know, I actually felt my heart go out in tenderness to this particular mother tabby and her mewing kits. It occurred to me, as she lay there, blinking and purring in apparent amiability and in evident pride, that here at least was a cat that would not kill birds; if so, I would adopt her, and as for the kittens — yes, I would adopt them, too.

I made up my mind that I would name the kittens after my most intimate neighbors; one should be Baylor, another Tiltman, another Rush, a fourth Denslow, the fifth Browe, and the sixth Roth. I am sorry there are not two more, for I should like to honor my two munificent patrons, Mr. Black and Mr. Rock. But there must be a limit to human possibilities. As for the mother cat herself, there was but one thing for me to do; I had to name her Alice, of course.

IX

NEIGHBOR MACLEOD'S THISTLE

THE incident of the tabby cat's appearance with six kittens may have been a
portent either of good or of evil. As you
know, I am not a superstitious person. I
smile at those whimsical fancies which figure
so conspicuously in many people's lives,
such as the howling of dogs, the flickering
of a candle, the arrangement of the grounds
in a cup, the cracking of a mirror, the sudden stopping of the clock, the crowing of
hens, the chirping of crickets, the hooting
of an owl, the fall of a family portrait, the
spilling of salt, a dream of the toothache,
etc., etc., etc. If this particular cat had
been black instead of tabby I should have
regarded her advent as a prognostic, for it
is conceded by all scientists that there is a
mysteriously subtle virtue in a black cat.

The fact, however, that she was tabby dispossessed her of all power either for evil or for good, and I could not help regarding Uncle Si with pity for the seeming veneration in which he held this harmless and innocent beast. Still I determined to watch and note events with a view to confuting the superstition which foresaw good luck in the presence of this cat and her offspring.

While the work of rehabilitating the old house was at its height I received a letter from my friend Byron Tinkle of Kansas City, congratulating me upon having secured so lovely a home after so many years of patient waiting. " And now," said he, "I am anxious to be represented by some bit of furniture in your new place. It has occurred to me that a handsome library table might be acceptable, and it would certainly delight me to present you with an object which would serve to remind you of your old schoolmate, whose affection for you has been abated neither by separation nor by the lapse of time."

Mr. Tinkle then went on to say that he had hit upon a very appropriate design for

a library table — a design full of historical
and mythological allusion. Four figures of
Atlas supporting the world were to serve as
the legs of this table. and around the sides
of the top were to be carved scenes illustrative of the progress of civilization since the
building of Solomon's temple. Upon the
four edges of the top were to be inlaid mo-
saic portraits of the most famous scientists,
including Æsculapius, Moses, Galileo, Dar-
win, Herschel, Mitchell, Huxley, Harvey,
Jenner, etc., and the top itself was to represent a cunningly devised map of the world.
in which my native town of Biddeford,
Maine. was to appear as the central and
most conspicuous figure.

I felt very grateful to my old friend Tinkle
for his generosity, but I said nothing of it to
Alice. Recalling the experience with Colonel Mullaly's yellow lamp, I suspected that
if Alice were to hear of this promised addition to our furniture she would surely change
the whole architectural scheme of our new
home in order to adapt it to the new centre
table.

Mr. Tinkle's princely offer was but the

beginning of a series of handsome and useful gifts. It seemed as if our friends no
sooner heard of our purchase of a home than
they became possessed of a desire to contribute toward embellishing that home.
Another Kansas City friend, Colonel Gustave
Gerton, late of the Bavarian Guards, tele-
graphed me that a dozen young apple trees,
carefully picked from his Nonpareil Nursery,
awaited my order. The Janowins, who
have a prosperous farm in Kentucky, duly
apprised us that when we were ready to
stock our place they would send us a heifer
and a litter of pigs. Cousin Jabez Fothergill forwarded to us all the way from Maine
a box which was found to contain a pint of
Hubbard squash seeds, a dozen daffodil
sprouts, and a goodly collection of catnip
roots. Offers of dogs came from numerous
quarters — dogs representing the mastiff,
bloodhound, Newfoundland, beagle, setter,
pointer, St. Bernard, terrier, bull, Spitz,
dachshund, spaniel, colly, pug, and poodle
families. Had we contemplated a peren-
nial bench show, instead of a quiet home,
we could hardly have been more favored.

With a discretion begotten of twenty years' experience as a husband, I referred all these proffers of canine gifts to Alice with power to act, and I dimly surmise that consideration of them has been postponed indefinitely.

As soon as our neighbors realized what horticultural possibilities our noble expanse of front yard offered they fairly overwhelmed us with floral and arboreal gifts. During that unusually warm spell we had about two months ago there was scarcely an hour of the day that a wheelbarrow or a man servant or both did not arrive bearing lilac sprouts from the Leets, or Japanese ivy slips from the Sissons, or peonies from the old Doller homestead, or mignonette from Mrs. Roth, or dahlias from Mrs. Knox, or marigolds from the Baylors, or pansies from the Haynes, or tulip bulbs from Mrs. Redd, or something or another from somebody else.

You can depend upon it that all this kept me wondrously busy. I broke four trowels and raised a dozen ugly blisters on my right hand in my attempt to get these tender tokens of friendship transplanted before they withered. One day Mrs. Baylor and Mrs. Rush took me to a neighboring greenhouse with them; they wanted to purchase some vines to train over their front porches. The man at the greenhouse showed me an innumerable assortment of beautiful rose-bushes, which I bought in the fond delusion that they would vastly embellish our front lawn. I recall the pride with which I told Alice and Adah that I guessed I had purchased enough flowers to fill the whole yard. I recall also the sense of humiliation I experienced when, after that innumerable assortment had been set out in the yard, I discovered that there was not enough of them to make an impression even upon the most susceptible eye.

I am not yet quite sure whether neighbor Macleod was in earnest or whether he meant it in fun when he sent us a magnificent this-tle, with the suggestion that we plant it in our lawn. But, out of respect to neighbor Macleod's patriotism as a loyal son of Cale-donia, I did plant the thistle in amiable com-pliance with my friend's suggestion. Other neighbors protested against this, but I imputed their objections to that natural feeling of jealousy which is too likely to manifest itself when the interests of other neighbors are involved. The thistle was an uncommonly large and active one, and I suffered somewhat from its teeth before I finally got it comfortably located in a patch of succulent turf under one of our willow-trees.

The unusually warm spell to which I have referred was followed (as you will doubtless recollect), by a period of bitterly cold weather. With an anguish which I am utterly incapable of describing, I saw my marigolds and mignonette and roses and peonies and dahlias and pansies and other leafy pets wither and droop and shrivel. In less than forty-eight hours' time they were all apparently as dead as that side of the moon which is invisible to us. The only flower or shrub in all that once blooming lawn which remained unshorn of its beauty by the bitter hyperborean blasts was the Macleod thistle. Proudly it reared itself amid that desolation, and defiantly it exhibited its fangs to foe and friend alike.

I cannot tell you how heartily I rejoiced

that I had not yielded to the importunities of the Baylors, the Tiltmans, the Browes, and the Denslows when, in an ebullition of neighborly jealousy, they sought the destruction of that sturdy plant. But my delight was of short duration. One morning before I arrived to pursue my horticultural avocation a remorseless policeman invaded the premises and pulled up the bristling emblem of Scotia and cast it into the hard highway under the pretext that by so doing he was complying with a provision of the revised statutes. I learned that this policeman is a Swede, and I can justify his conduct only upon the hypothesis of heredity, although it is hard to conceive that the malignant feeling which existed centuries ago among the Norsemen who were wont to harry the Scottish coast should exhibit itself at this remote period in the demeanor of a naturalized Swede who presumably does not know the difference between a viking and a meteorite.

If I had been of a sarcastic or of a bitter nature, I might have imputed this curious train of mishaps to the malign influence of that maternal tabby cat which Uncle Si had hailed as a harbinger of good luck. As it was, I could not resist giving play to my desire for retaliation when Uncle Si confided to me one morning that some unscrupulous person or persons had invaded the premises the night before and had carried off about six thousand feet of choice lumber. I was disposed to be very wroth at first, but when I gathered from Uncle Si's remarks that the loss would fall upon him and not upon me my anger was assuaged to a degree that admitted of my suggesting to Uncle Si that perhaps this incident might be reckoned as a part of that " good luck " which the advent of the tabby cat and her kits had prognosticated.

Having unbosomed myself of this perhaps too savage thrust, I gave Uncle Si a cigar and in my most cordial tones bade him "never mind and be of good cheer." I make it a practice never to say or do that which is likely to occasion pain or humiliation without accompanying the word or the deed with somewhat that shall serve as an antidote thereunto. For I bear ill will to none, and it is constantly my endeavor to make life pleasant and dear not only to myself but also to my fellow beings.

My consideration for Uncle Si's feelings was almost immediately rewarded, for as I left Uncle Si smoking his cigar in a comforted mood I beheld my neighbor, Colonel Bobbett Doller, coming up the driveway and beckoning to me. If you know the colonel as I do, you know him to be a gentleman of wealth, of position, and of influence. Moreover, Colonel Doller is a man of large sympathies. He had heard of our recent acquisition and had come to congratulate me. We shook hands warmly.

" You have here," said Colonel Doller, cordially, "a magnificent property, and I heartily rejoice to learn that you acquired it at a merely nominal price. Has it occurred to you, my dear sir, that this tract, with its majestic sweep of lawn and its picturesque glory of shade trees, presents tremendous possibilities — in fact, secures to you the opportunity of comprehending riches beyond the dreams of avarice? Let us be seated upon this pile of bricks while I unfold to you a panorama of potentialities."

X

COLONEL DOLLER'S GREAT IDEA

COLONEL BOBBETT DOLLER and I sat
down, side by side, on the pile of bricks,
and the colonel proceeded straightway to
disclose pleasing visions to my mind's eye.

" You are doubtless aware," said the colonel, "that you are not, in the severest ac-
ceptation of the term, a business man?"

"Alas," said I, "I am compelled in all
candor to admit that lamentable fact."

"Then," continued the colonel, "you
probably do not know that this noble expanse of high ground upon which your
stately residence is reared is the exact centre
of a radius of eighty miles.   In other words,
did the power of your vision extend eighty
miles you would be able to see for yourself
from the roof of your superb house that this

point is in fact the centre of a radius representing a stretch in any and every direction of eighty miles."

"No, I had never supposed it possible," said I.

"It is, nevertheless, a demonstrable fact," said Colonel Doller. "It is more notorious, however, that this property of yours (designated in the records as the south half of lot 16, Terhune's addition, section 9, township of Pond View) "——

"Page 273, volume 105," said I, interrupting him; for I suddenly recalled the superscription on the warranty deed.

"Exactly," said Colonel Doller, with a genial smile. "Now, as I was about to remark, it is notorious that this property of yours is situate in the very heart of the delectable tract known to the world as the North Shore. I do not exaggerate when I say, in the language of my popular brochure entitled, 'Homes for the Homeless,' that the North Shore offers inducements, both for the living and for the dead, which are not met with in any other part of our growing community. Recognizing the merit of these inducements, immigration has turned its tide toward the North Shore. Ten years ago there was naught but desolation where now the dandelion blooms and the voice of the tree-toad is heard in song. What do we see about us to-day? To the north of us the roof of Martin Howard's new barn glistens under the smiling noonday sun. Turning our gaze westward we behold the turrets of the palatial residence which neighbor Bales has erected in Razzle Street. Yonder in the southeast horizon we detect the tall, lithe flagpole which Major Ryson has set up as a graceful tribute to the memory of the late lamented yacht club. Cast your eyes where you will and you will see convincing evidences of the onward, irresistible march of civilization.

" This noble property of yours," continued Colonel Doller, " is the very heart of all this pulsing, throbbing, bustling, teeming civilization. Why, my dear Baker, I would not exchange (if I were you) the opportunities now within your grasp for any other conceivable thing — not even though millions were placed in the opposing scale!"

"I don't believe I understand you," said I.

"I will be more explicit," said Colonel Doller. "The tide of immigration has already overwhelmed this section; a great commercial wave is closely following it. Trade will soon locate its emporiums in the midst of us. Already two blocks to the south of this property a commercial mart has begun to invite the attention and the patronage of our public."

"You refer to Pusheck's grocery store?"

"The same," said Colonel Doller. "Presently a barber-shop and a banana stand will follow: then a bicycle repair-shop will spring up in our midst, and from that moment our status as a commercial centre will be assured."

As I was in no sense a business man I could not deny this. To be frank with you, it all looked very plausible to me.

"There is nothing else," continued Colonel Doller, "more practicable or of greater value than foreseeing events and being prepared for them. Now, here you are in the very midst of this flood of immigration, and with the tidal wave of commerce at your very door.

Is your property in a position to avail you
handsomely in case you accede to the demands of reason and conclude to yield to the
persuasions of immigration and commerce?
The consideration which should be paramount with you is this: 'Having secured
this property, how can I get rid of it to the
best advantage?'"

"But it is n't for sale," said I.

"True, quite true," answered Colonel Doller, with a weary, patient smile, "but it will
be. What is North Shore property for if not
for sale? You certainly do not intend to vio-
late all the customs and traditions of the community by holding out against an opportunity to benefit yourself? That, my dear
Baker, would be folly."

"But nobody has asked us to sell," said
I, apologetically.

"That is because your property is not in
desirable shape," said the colonel. "If it
were, you would have chances to enrich
yourself in less than a month. You see your
lot fronts one hundred feet on Clarendon
Avenue, and runs back two hundred and
thirty-nine feet to a prospective alley; this

gives you one hundred feet of salable property, but with a depth that actually involves
a wicked waste of land. Now suppose you
were to buy the twenty-five feet that lies to
the south on Clarendon Avenue just between
your lot and Sandpile Terrace. That would
give you a frontage of two hundred and
thirty-nine feet on the terrace, with a depth
altogether of one hundred and twenty-five
feet! Do you follow me?"

"Yes, I see," said I, as this good and
shrewd man's meaning gradually stole upon
me.

"With that additional twenty-five feet,"
resumed Colonel Doller, "you could divide
up the whole property into what you might
call (if you chose) Baker's Subdivision: then
you could parcel it off into twenty-foot lots
with frontage on Sandpile Terrace — and
there you are, a rich man almost before you
know it."

"Gracious me! That *is* a great idea!"
said I, and I whistled softly to myself.

"Great? Well, I should say so!" exclaimed Colonel Doller. "I knew it would
appeal to you, for you are a man of intelli-

gence and capable of foreseeing and appre-
ciating potentialities."

"Who owns that strip?" I asked, referring to the twenty-five feet adjoining our lot
to the south.

"Well, it happens to be mine," said Colonel Doller. "As soon as I heard that you
had purchased this place it occurred to me
that you ought to have that twenty-five feet
in order to make the rest of your property
available. So, without saying a word about
it to anybody else, I've stepped over here to
tell you that if you want it I'll throw that
strip in to you at one hundred and twenty-
five dollars per front foot."

"We gave only one hundred dollars a
foot for this lot," said I.

"Very true," said Colonel Doller, "but
my lot admits of giving you a frontage of
two hundred and thirty-nine feet on Sandpile Terrace."

"To be sure it does," said I. "For the
moment I quite lost sight of that. Well, I
think very favorably of it, and I suspect Mr.
Black would insist upon my closing with
you at once. I'll speak to Alice about it."

"Be careful not to breathe a word of it to anybody else," suggested Colonel Doller in a low, mysterious tone, "and whatever else you do, don't let my partner, Leet, have even so much as an inkling of the fact that we 've had a talk! You understand?"

"It shall be kept a profound secret!" said I, with solemn earnestness.

Colonel Doller patted me reassuringly on the shoulder as he arose to depart.

"Baker," said he, kindly, "you are as good as a rich man already! You get that extra twenty-five feet and make a subdivision of this property, and you 'll have so much money you won't know what to do with it! Why, the next thing we 'll hear of you, you 'll be living in a castle on a hill, with an observatory — just think of it, Baker, old man! an observatory and a twelve-foot telescope capable of discovering a new comet every night, rain or shine!"

The kind gentleman's enthusiasm quite took my breath away. As I watched him departing down the shady drive my heart overflowed with gratitude, and again I thanked the providential Power that had given me so many kind, solicitous, and self-sacrificing friends.

My conversation with Colonel Doller set me to indulging in thoughts which were entirely new to me, and which pleased me with their novelty and brilliancy. I fancied myself already possessed of a wealth which permitted me to pursue unreservedly those studies and investigations which have been my delight since youth. In imagination I pictured myself the owner of a sightly residence surmounted by a spacious observatory, in which was located a magnificent reflector-telescope operated by the newest and nicest mechanism. It was pleasing to be rich, even in fancy. My thoughts reverted to the children.

"Dear pampered darlings," I murmured, "they little know the lives of independence and of ease that are before them. They will never know what it is to toil and to economize. And Alice—sweet girl—this will put an end to her worry about grocery bills!"

It is curious how completely I lost interest in our new house as soon as the prospect

of getting rich dawned upon me. You will
not believe it, but after that talk with Colonel
Doller I looked with actual disdain upon the
old Schmittheimer home and its broad, vel-
vety lawn under the noble trees. I was so
possessed with the fascinating scheme suggested by Colonel Doller that I was even
tempted to bid Uncle Si and his men quit
work until I had consulted with Alice as to
the feasibility of abandoning the proposed
improvements and investing the rest of Mr.
Black's three thousand dollars in the twenty-
five-foot strip to the south of us. I am glad
now that the still small voice within me prevailed, and that I saw Alice before saying
anything to Uncle Si.

"Reuben Baker," exclaimed Alice, "that
property is *mine* and I bought it for a home,
not to *sell*. If you and Colonel Doller want
to speculate, you need n't think you 're going to rope me into any of your schemes."

"But, Alice, darling—"

"I sha' n't listen to a word of such non-
sense," persisted Alice. "So, there."

I was inclined to remonstrate, but just at
that moment the front door bell rang and a

telegraphic message was handed in. The message was from Cincinnati and it read in this wise:

"Shall be there to-morrow morning to look things over.   *Luther M. Black.*"

In the prospect of a visit from our patron, Mr. Black, I speedily forgot all about Colonel Bobbett Doller and his pleasing panorama of potentialities. In this we see illustrated the wisdom of Providence in so dispensing human events as to soothe the wounds of disappointment with the balm of anticipation.

XI

I MAKE A STAND FOR MY RIGHTS

SHORTLY after Mr. Black's arrival that worthy gentleman was escorted with all due formality to the old Schmittheimer place in Clarendon Avenue. Recognizing the fact that first impressions are lasting, we determined that Mr. Black's first impressions of our purchase should be favorable. So we conducted him to our property by a rather circuitous route. The approach to the old Schmittheimer place from the north is by all means the most agreeable; it leads by Mr. Rink's fine colonial house and Martin Howard's new place and through an embowered avenue of weeping willows, which, out of deference to his melancholy profession, Mr. Dimmons, landscape gardener of our most prosperous cemetery, has constructed in front of his beautiful residence in Thistle

Patch Court; a turn is then made upon Dandelion Place, and just one block this side of Mr. Allworth's bowlder house (famous as the greatest bargain ever acquired on the North Shore) another turn to the right brings you in sight and within a few yards of our property.

Mr. Black was pleased with the neighborhood. He is not a man of enthusiasms; in all the years of my acquaintance with him I have never known him to give way to an ebullition of any kind. Yet upon this occasion there was an expression upon his face when he first set eyes upon our property which gave me to understand that he approved of our purchase. I hastened to clinch this favorable impression by apprising him briefly of the proposition Colonel Bobbett Doller had made to me the previous afternoon, and I flatter myself that, between us, Alice and I made a pretty fair presentation of the merits of our new place.

" You seem to have begun reconstructing the house," said Mr. Black. " Who is your architect ? "

" We have no real architect," said I. " In

order to save expense we have employed a boss carpenter capable not only of designing plans, but also of executing them. His name is Silas Plum."

"Plum? That is a very familiar name to me," said Mr. Black. "I wonder whether he is any kin to the Plum family of Maine. There was an Elnathan Plum, who used to live in Aroostook, and I went to school with him at Pocatapaug Academy in the winter of 1827. The last time I visited Maine I was told that he had moved west in 1840, or thereabouts. He married a third cousin of mine whose maiden name was Eastman — Euphemia Eastman, as I recall it."

Of course I was unable to say what Uncle Si's antecedents were, but I felt pretty certain that, if left to himself, Mr. Black would find out all about them, for of all the people I ever met with Mr. Black surely has the most astounding faculty for acquiring and remembering genealogical data.

Our worthy friend consumed fully a half-hour's time inspecting our front lawn, examining into the condition of the fence, learning what kind of trees we had, and ascertaining the character and depth of the soil. I do not hesitate to affirm that he knew more about these things at the end of that half-hour than I shall know at the end of ten years' daily association with them. I took pains, however, to make the most of what small knowledge I had, and with considerable flourish I called Mr. Black's attention to our lilac and gooseberry bushes, and with conscious pride pointed out the wild grape vine in the corner of the yard. I told Mr. Black that it was our intention to have a kitchen garden back of the house, and that among other things we should cultivate onions of the choicest quality. I had an object in specifying the onions particularly, for I knew that Mr. Black had a fondness (amounting almost to a passion) for this succulent fruit.

In all that I pointed out and in all that I said Mr. Black appeared to take more than common interest. One thing that seemed to please him particularly was the discovery that three of our currant bushes had escaped the malice of the workmen, and he promised Alice to write to his niece at Biddeford for her recipe for making currant wine, a beverage which, he assured us. would cheer but not inebriate.

Alice and I had made it up beforehand that we would leave Mr. Black and Uncle Si together for a spell after we had introduced them to each other; for we wanted our patron to learn for himself (unembarrassed by our presence) just what had been done and how it had been done. I take it for granted that the two enjoyed their three hours' confabulation, but I more than half suspect they spent precious little of that time in a discussion of our affairs. Mr. Black told me afterward that he had ascertained that Uncle Si (or Silas, as he called him) was, as he had surmised, a son of Elnathan Plum of Aroostook.

"Silas looks more like his mother's side of the family," said Mr. Black. "The Eastmans, as I remember them, were tall and spare, with blue eyes and straight noses. We have an Eastman in Cincinnati who looks enough like Silas to be his brother, although he belongs to the Ebenezer Eastman branch of the family, who located in Westboro, Mass.. in 1765. Tooker Eastman, the

Cincinnati representative of the family, is pastor of the First Church; he married Sukey, the widow of Amos Sears, who (that is to say, Amos) was a son of Calvin Sears, who was postmaster at Biddeford while I was a young man in that town."

From this and other similar morsels of information which Mr. Black let fall in my hearing I gathered that Mr. Black's talk with Uncle Si had been rather of a historical and reminiscent than of a business character. But this mattered not to me; it was clear that Mr. Black approved of our purchase and of the improvements we contemplated, and that was enough to insure our entire satisfaction.

When I came down from my study that evening I found Mr. Black and Alice sitting in the parlor, looking mysteriously solemn.

"I have been advising your wife to make a will," said Mr. Black.

"Why, Alice dear, are you ill?" I asked, in genuine alarm.

Alice laughingly answered that she had never before felt heartier or in finer spirits.

"Then why make a will?" I asked.

"Who ever heard of a person's making a will unless he was sick?"

"You are laboring under a delusion too common to humanity," said Mr. Black. "In the midst of life we are in death. It is during health and while we are in full possession of our physical and mental faculties that we should provide against that penalty which we all alike as debtors are sooner or later to pay to nature. Your wife has recently become possessed by purchase of property that may eventually be of large value. It seems proper that she should draw a will indicating her desires as to the disposal of this property in the event of her demise."

"But what," I cried with honest feeling, "what would be lands or gold without my Alice?"

"Calm your agitation, Reuben dear," said Alice. "The suggestion which Mr. Black has made does not involve you to the extent of making you an heir."

"No," said Mr. Black, "it is proper that you should have a life estate in the property, but the property itself should ultimately go to the children."

"Still," said Alice, thoughtfully, "if Reuben were to survive me it would be just like him to marry again, and I believe I should just rise up in my grave if I thought another woman was living on the premises which I myself had earned."

"Oh, but Alice, that is very unfair!" I expostulated. "It is *I* who am earning the money — or, at least, it is I who expect to earn the money wherewith to repay our dear friend, Mr. Black, the sums he has advanced and may advance for our property!"

"There! I suspected it all the time," cried Alice, indignantly. "You are already claiming the property — you are already preparing for my death — I daresay you have your eyes already on the woman who is to step into my place when I am gone! But I won't die — no, I just won't! But I 'll make a will and I 'll give everything to the children, and you sha'n't have a thing when I do die — not a thing, not even a life estate — so there!"

Mr. Black and I were trying to soothe the dear creature, when there came a knock at the front door. Alice popped up and made her escape into the dining-room. The front door opened and the ruddy, smiling face of neighbor Denslow appeared.

"Pardon my informality," said Mr. Denslow, cheerily; "can I come in?"

"By all means," I cried. "You are in good season to meet my old and valued friend, Mr. Black."

Mr. Denslow greeted Mr. Black effusively. All my neighbors had heard me speak of my generous patron, and they all took a really noble neighborly pride in promoting my interests with him. Mr. Denslow began at once to dilate in eloquent terms upon the bargain Alice and I had secured in the old Schmittheimer place.

"And, by the way," said Mr. Denslow, turning to me, "the mention of your bargain reminds me of the object of my call. August Schmittheimer, a son of the widow, came to my office to-day to tell me that he is prepared to let you have the thirty-three feet in the rear of your lot at a merely nominal price — say two hundred dollars.

I had cast envious eyes upon this particular strip of ground several times. Alice had remarked that it would afford an ideal spot upon which to hang out the washing on Monday mornings; at other times it would serve as a convenient playground for Josephine and little Erasmus. It really seemed like a special Providence that what we had been wishing for should unexpectedly be thrust within our very grasp.

"I think that we should have that extra strip by all means," said I; and then I added, by way of demonstrating the wisdom of my opinion to Mr. Black: "We shall thus be enabled to enlarge our onion bed to pretentious proportions."

This argument must have convinced Mr. Black, for he remarked at once that he recognized the wisdom of acquiring the extra piece of land at the bargain price suggested.

"If it pleases you, then," said Mr. Denslow, "I will attend the first thing in the morning to having the investigation into the title begun, and I suppose that within the next three days the deal can be consummated and the property duly transferred to Mrs. Baker."

Too often I do not think of the bright and

felicitous thing to say or do until it is too late. On this occasion, however, a really shrewd and happy thought occurred to me. The somewhat malicious purpose it contemplated was justified, I claim, by the context (so to speak) of events.

"Neighbor Denslow," said I, confidentially, "when it comes to the transfer of that property please be so kind as to have the warranty deed made to me."

Mr. Denslow looked so surprised, and so did Mr. Black, that I deemed an explanation necessary.

XII

I AM DECEIVED IN MR. WAX

I WENT on to say that it seemed to me to be unwise to invest too much power in Alice's hands; that *I* had certain rights which should be protected, and that if I was not to be assured a life estate in Alice's property I ought to have at least thirty-three feet to which I could, in an emergency, retire to spend the evening of my existence in peace and security.

"Possessed of that thirty-three feet," said I, "I make no question that I shall soon be able to bring Alice to terms. Give me the power to stand on my own patch of ground and defy Alice every Monday morning when the weekly wash is ready to be hung out, and I will cheerfully risk the future."

Mr. Denslow and Mr. Black are sensible and loyal men: they recognized the propriety of standing by me in this emergency, and it was agreed that the extra piece of ground should be conveyed to me.

That night I dreamed that Alice had been called to her heavenly reward and that I had been turned out of doors by our heartless children. I was an aged and tottering man. The wind blew lustily and a storm was raging. I drew my threadbare coat closer about me, for I was shivering with the cold.

"Alas," I cried (in my dream), "whither shall I turn? Is there no spot on earth where I can die in peace?"

Then, O joy! it occurred to me (in my dream) that I owned the thirty-three feet back of the dear old home. Two years' taxes were due on it, but it was still mine--- all mine!

"The snow is deep and clean and hospitable there," I cried (still in my dream), "and it is all mine own! To that snowbank will I make my way, and there will I lie down to sleep my last sleep."

But just then I awoke to discover that it was only a dream. Had I been of a superstitious nature I might have read in this

dream divers premonitions and strange sig-
nificances. As it was, it merely confirmed
me in my belief that I had done wisely in securing that thirty-three-foot strip.

Mr. Black went back home next day, and
nothing more was said for the nonce about
a " will " or a "life estate," or any matter
thereunto appertaining, and disagreeable to
Alice and to me alike. The cold weather
having melted away into sunshine and
warmth, I once more began to be deeply interested in horticulture and floriculture,
and this, too, in spite of the ineffaceable
scars which the spade-wielding vandals had
left in the large front yard in the alleged interest of the sewer, water, and gas-pipes.

This enthusiasm of mine in behalf of matters of which I knew absolutely nothing was
refired by my respected neighbor, Fadda
Pierce, who is so learned in all affairs involving flowers and shrubbery that I actually believe that what he does n't know about them
is n't worth knowing. Fadda's cottage is
covered with every variety of dainty and
luxurious vine, and in his yard bloom all
kinds of rare and beautiful flowers. He is

so famed for his fondness for and luck with
flowers that I felt grateful to the dear old
gentleman when he visited me with a view
to advising me as to the kind of flowers I
ought to plant in my lawn and around the
house.   ·

It was then that I learned of the existence
of shrubs, vines, and flowers of which I had
never before heard. It is indeed amazing
that an ordinarily intelligent man can reach
the age of forty-five years without being able
to profess truthfully a more or less intimate
acquaintance with hydrangeas, fuchsias,
taraxacums, syringas, sisymbriums, gilli-
flowers, kentaphyllons, maydenheer, chrys-
anthemums, orchids, geraniums, lichens,
laburnums, jasmines, heliotropes, gentians,
eucalyptuses, crocuses, carnations, dahlias,
cactuses, billybuttons, anemones, anthropo-
morphons, amaranths, etc. etc.   Fadda
Pierce did not chide me for my heathenish
ignorance; he seemed to take it for granted
that I had been too busy acquiring knowledge in other lines to have time to devote
to research in botany.   He was much more
considerate than neighbor Roth was when

he pulled up his team in front of my house one day and asked me how far it was to Glencoe. I answered that I did not know; whereupon he shrugged his shoulders and muttered: "I thought as much, by gosh! You can tell how fur 't is to the sun, the moon, an' the stars, but you can't tell how fur 't is to Glencoe!"

Fadda Pierce advised me to set out about two dozen cobies (I think he called them) around our new colonial front porch, and then he kindly designated certain spots in the yard where beds ought to be constructed for certain flowers, the names of which he wrote down on a slip of paper. Some of these beds were to be circular, some square, and some oblong. Fadda told me that I would require at least three loads of black dirt, and he gave me the address of a person who dealt in this precious commodity at one dollar and a half a load. I called upon this person at once and ordered the three loads of black dirt to be delivered immediately. I then bethought myself that I required an outfit of garden tools; so I made my way to the nearest hardware shop and purchased a spade, a hoe, a rake, a wheelbarrow, a watering can, a trowel, and a pruning-knife. I trundled the barrow home, with the other purchases in it.

The day was exceedingly warm, and my appearance in this new rôle excited the derision of my neighbors; but I felt rather flattered to be called Farmer Baker, and I was glad to give the Baylors, the Edwardses, the Dollers, the Tiltmans, the Rushes, the Sissons, and the rest to understand that I by no means disdained to condescend to the humble plane of an agriculturist. Now that I come to think of it, I remember to have read somewhere that Galileo took his recreation at hoeing and grubbing in the vineyard adjoining his observatory.

As I trundled the barrow up the winding road of the Schmittheimer place I became aware that a man was following me. So I stopped and waited for him to overtake me. His appearance indicated poverty and all its attendant miseries.

"Good sir," said the stranger, "pardon me for this intrusion, but misfortunes of a most grievous character compel me to thrust myself upon your mercy. You behold in me, sir, one of the most hapless of creatures, one whom adversity has buffeted with cruel pertinacity, and finally driven out to become a homeless and friendless wanderer upon the face of the earth. My name, sir, is Percival Wax, born and reared under the auspices of riches, but now forced by the reverses of remorseless fate to importune you for the wherewithal to procure food and lodging.''

"Mr. Wax," said I, " your appearance by no means belies your words. Your raiment is torn and soiled; your shoes are not mates, and your hat was evidently made for a larger head than yours. I also read in your dim eyes, your unkempt beard, and your dishevelled hair corroboration of your claims to intimacy with adversity. While I sympathize with you in your misfortune, I cannot break one of the imperative rules which govern the conduct of my life; if you are willing to work I will gladly provide you with the means of relief from your embarrassment."

"Work? Ah, kind sir," said Mr. Wax, eagerly, "it is that which I have vainly sought for weeks. I have been out of employment ever since the combined efforts of our National Administration and of our incompetent Congress succeeded in sowing the seeds of distrust in every mind, thereby stagnating business and precipitating a financial crisis, from the débris of which I can never hope to arise."

"Can you make flower-beds, Mr. Wax?" I asked.

"Kind gentleman," he answered, "my profession before financial ruin overwhelmed me was that of a landscape gardener."

This was, indeed, a marvellously pleasing coincidence. Here was the very man I needed.

"Take up the barrow, Mr. Wax, and follow me," said I.

I showed him where I wanted the flower-beds made—the circular, the square, and the oblong. He was first to remove the turf and then fill in and square up the beds with black dirt. I found him quick to understand, and he seemed to be anxious to get to work.

"You can begin as soon as you please,"

said I. "Meanwhile I shall go to luncheon, and on my return I shall bring you three or four mustard sandwiches and some hard-boiled eggs to stay you until you have finished your task."

"Thank you, kind sir," said Mr. Wax with tears of gratitude in his voice.

I was gone an hour or more. At luncheon I told Alice of what I had done, but she did not seem to share my enthusiasm at having provided Mr. Wax with an opportunity to turn an honest penny or two. She very clearly indicated to me her distrust of all tramps, to which class she was sure Mr. Wax belonged. Thereupon I warned Alice against the inhumanity and wickedness of insensibility to the sufferings of others, and I was glad that the children were at the table with us to hear my remarks in praise of that charity which has compassion for all conditions of misery.

Upon my return to the Schmittheimer place I was disappointed to find that no progress had been made with the flower-beds.

"I wonder where Mr. Wax is?" said I to Uncle Si.

"Do you mean that —— tramp that was here about noon?" asked Uncle Si.

"He may have been a tramp," said I, purposely ignoring Uncle Si's profane epithet (for I do not approve of profanity).

"He went away shortly after you went," said Uncle Si. "I asked him where he was going with the wheelbarrow and the garden tools, and he said you had hired him to take them over to your house in Heavenward Avenue for you."

"Mr. Wax lied to you," said I. "He has stolen that barrow and those tools."

Uncle Si consoled me by telling me that in all human probability Mr. Wax had sold his stealings by this time and was already squandering his ill-gotten gains in a barroom. I lamented not only the ingratitude and dishonesty of this man whom I had sought to befriend, but also the loss of my barrow and my garden tools. There was, however, some consolation in the thought that my experience would serve me to good purpose in the future.

The three mustard sandwiches and the two hard-boiled eggs which I had brought from home for Mr. Wax's luncheon I now took down into the cellar and fed to Alice, the mother cat. Had I been a superstitious person I should not have performed this kind deed by one whom many might have regarded as the prognostic (if not actually the cause) of the many evils which had befallen me of late. As it was, I took a kind of spiteful satisfaction in observing that the gaunt beast did not exhibit that exuberant fondness for mustard sandwiches and hard-boiled eggs which might be confidently looked for in the mother of six healthy and always hungry kittens.

XIII

EDITOR WOODSIT A TRUE FRIEND

ONE morning — it was a Thursday morning, as I distinctly recall — I was much surprised to find that work upon the house had practically been suspended. I was sure there could not have been a strike, for I told the workmen at the beginning that whenever they felt as if they were not getting enough pay they must come to me about it and I would raise their wages. They had already been to me three times and received an increase of pay each time. So I felt moderately secure against a strike. Uncle Si explained the situation briefly.

"The plasterers were to have begun today," said he, "but there is no water for them; so I had to send them away."

"No water?" I cried. "No water? Then

tell me, I pray, why this noble front yard of ours has been converted into a dreary waste by those vandals with their spades and picks? Why is that deep, wide, ragged ditch still yawning in our faces and threatening the death of every tree at whose roots it crawls? And why did I pay Sibley the plumber forty-five dollars last Saturday night, if it were not for the laying of water pipe in that hideous ditch? No water, indeed!"

"It is nobody's fault but the city's," explained Uncle Si. "The pipe is all laid and nothing remains but for the city to make the connection with the main in the street. You see *we* can't tap the main; that is for the city to do."

"Then why does n't the city do it?" I asked.

Uncle Si shrugged his shoulders.

"The city *ought* to do a good many things it *does n't* do," said he. "They promised to have that main tapped at eight o'clock last Monday morning, and here it is ten o'clock Thursday morning and not a drop of water on the place! There is n't any use kicking, for those politicians down at the City

Hall do things their own way and take their own time doing 'em!"

I saw that argument with Uncle Si meant simply a waste of time, so I determined to go down-town to the City Hall myself to see whether no eloquence or indignation of my own would move the derelict officers to a performance of their duty. On the train I fell in with Mr. Leet, who was on his way to his place of business. He had not seen me since our purchase of the Schmittheimer property, and he took this first occasion to congratulate me upon what he called one of those bargains which occur at rare intervals in a century. Finding me in a felicitous mood, Mr. Leet went on to say that the property we already possessed would be enhanced in value an hundred-fold and would be rendered marketable instantaneously by the further acquisition of the twenty-five feet adjoining it upon the north.

"Yes," said I, "Mr. Doller spoke to me about that twenty-five-foot strip some time ago."

"Aha, so Doller has been approaching you, has he?" said Mr. Leet, softly. "Well,

Doller is very cunning — very cunning, indeed. But he has nothing to do with the *north* strip. *He* owns the twenty-five feet to the *south* of your property, the piece fronting on Sandpile Terrace, and a very malarious location it is, too. I pledge you my word, Mr. Baker, I have seen mosquitos hovering over that Doller strip at night as big as bats!"

I could neither deny nor affirm the truth of this assertion.

"My twenty-five-foot strip to the north," continued Mr. Leet, "is high and dry and sightly. The view it commands of the Water Works is indescribably fine. You are surely practical enough to see, Mr. Baker, that by purchasing that strip and throwing it in with yours you will have a subdivision fronting upon Dandelion Place which would offer unparalleled inducements to the seeker after suburban property. What is more," added Mr. Leet in a confidential whisper, "it would not surprise me a bit if there were coal deposits in the twenty-five-foot strip of mine. I have very distinct suspicions, but the paramount importance of my other business interests has prevented me from making the investigation which might enrich me beyond all calculation. Now, you have time, and if you feel disposed to take that property I'll let you have it at the merely nominal price of one hundred and twenty-five dollars a front foot."

This seemed reasonable enough, particularly when I considered the chances of there being a coal mine on the property. However, as I had told Mr. Doller, so I now told Mr. Leet: I would first have to speak to Alice about the matter. Then I confided to Mr. Leet the object of my mission down-town. Presumably in the hope of insuring and clinching my devotion to his interests as represented in his twenty-five-foot lot, Mr. Leet manifested solicitude in my behalf and inveighed bitterly against the shiftlessness of the municipal administration as illustrated in the neglect to tap the water main for the benefit of my property.

"The most aggravatingly exasperating part of it all," says I, "is that I am a Republican and have been one for thirty years. Moreover, I am a reformer, having helped to organize the Civic Federation and having served for somewhat more than a year as chairman of the Special Committee on Ash Barrels and Garbage Boxes in the third precinct of the Twenty-fifth Ward. I made several addresses during the last campaign in advocacy of civil-service reform and all those other reforms which are invariably advocated and promised by the party which is not in power but wants to be. In the thirty years that I have been a Republican I have never asked a favor of my party, and it does seem just a bit ungrateful that the Republican reform municipal administration which I helped to elect should seize with apparent avidity upon its first opportunity to snub me by refusing to tap the public water main in front of my property."

"You should see Mayor Speedy about it," suggested Mr. Leet.

"I thought of doing so," said I, "but as I had already determined to approach him with reference to changing the name of Mush Street to Clarendon Avenue, I concluded that I ought not to call upon him with this complaint about the water. I particularly wish to avoid all appearance of hampering the administration with importunities and complaints of a personal nature."

"A man of your reputation," said Mr. Leet, "should certainly have the strongest kind of a pull at the City Hall."

"You may not believe it," said I, "but I do not know a man in the City Hall. I visit the place but twice a year, and my dealings on those occasions are restricted to a haughty young foreigner, who graciously permits me to pay him the amount of my water tax and then waves me to another foreigner who in turn waves me to the door. No, I have no influence at the City Hall, and as I was telling Editor Woodsit last week —"

"Do you know Editor Woodsit?" asked Mr. Leet, interrupting me.

"Indeed I do." said I; "he has promised to print my essay on the nebular hypothesis of Professor Lecouvrier as soon as his contract with the monometallist college professors expires. He is one of the most intimate friends I have."

"Then he is just the one to fix that City Hall matter for you," said Mr. Leet.

"Woodsit is the most potent political influence in the midst of us."

It was hard to understand why a potent political influence should be invoked in order to secure the tapping of a water main. However, I determined to enlist the coöperation of my journalistic friend. Twenty or thirty people were waiting outside Editor Woodsit's door. This number included noted clergymen, poets, authors, politicians, jurists, merchants, etc., etc. By some means or another, Editor Woodsit learned I was among the waiting throng, and he sent for me to come in. His private office is spacious and elegantly furnished. The walls are hung with splendid tapestries and costly oil paintings. Over Editor Woodsit's desk appears the legend, " The Pen Is Mightier Than the Sword." Near the desk are rows of nickel-plated tubes, about six feet in height and two feet in diameter; the lids or covers to these tubes are opened by means of a keyboard in front of the editor. The tubes themselves contain the heads of the departments of the State and municipal governments.

"What you tell me pains me deeply," said Mr. Woodsit, after he heard my story. "But there is no need of going to the City Hall about it; the matter can be attended to here. I never trifle with underlings when the responsible heads are at hand."

Editor Woodsit reached over and touched a button on the keyboard; it was button No. 9. Immediately the lid or top of tube No. 9 flew open and the head and face of a man appeared; it was the head and face of Commissioner Dent.

" This friend of mine," said Editor Woodsit, sternly, "complains that he can't get your department to connect the pipe with the water main in front of his property. My friend is a Republican, Dent, and he is a reformer. What excuse have you to offer for neglecting him ?"

Commissioner Dent turned very pale and he vainly tried to stammer an apology.

" This is a pretty kind of reform !" cried Editor Woodsit, savagely. " If a similar complaint occurs again I shall have your case investigated by my legal and spiritual counsellor, Joshua Selah, and may be have you impeached. Now see that Mr. Baker's reasonable demands are complied with at once.

With these words Editor Woodsit touched another button, and the head and face of Commissioner Dent disappeared and the top closed down over the box. It was all the work of two or three minutes, and it was certainly the most marvellous experience I had ever met with. My wonderment increased when I learned an hour later, upon my arrival home, that less than fifteen minutes (as I figure it) after I left Editor Woodsit's office an employé of Commissioner Dent's department came galloping up to my place on a foam-flecked steed, and, vaulting from his saddle, unswung his melting-furnace, soldering-irons, and other tools, and, quicker than you could say a pater noster, tapped the water main and made the desired connection with the pipe that fed my premises.

"I guess you must have a pull at the City Hall," said Uncle Si; and then he went on to tell me how people who have no pull have to wait weeks, sometimes, before their just requirements are answered by the municipal authorities.   If what Uncle Si tells me is true I cannot be too glad that I have what is even more efficacious than a pull at the City Hall — a friend in Editor Woodsit.

XIV

THE VICTIM OF AN ORDINANCE.

AND now that a plentiful supply of water was provided, it seemed proper to celebrate by giving the lawn (poor abused thing!) a deluge of the refreshing element. The exceeding ardor of the sun and the absence of rain had wrought havoc with the grass and shrubbery. The drought seemed determined to finish the work of destruction which the workmen, with their picks and spades, had begun. With a joyous heart, therefore, I applied myself to the task of rescuing the fainting vegetation. I borrowed Mr. Tiltman's hose because it was the best and longest in the neighborhood and was provided with a patent nozzle which was so versatile that there was actually no detail in its business which it did not perform in a most masterly way. I shall never forget the feeling of exultation with which I stood on that expansive lawn and sprayed the parched grass and drooping shrubbery. I fancied I could see the thirsty blades and leaves reach up to drink in the restoring element. My thoughts while I was thus engaged were similar, I suppose, to those of benevolent men who hasten to the succor of their suffering fellow-beings. I can imagine that it was with some such inspiring feelings that relief was borne to Livingstone in Africa and to Greely in the Arctic Circle. To the good man it is always a pleasure to do an act of magnanimity, and the fact that my considerate regard for our lawn involved no danger or privation did not serve in the least to abate my satisfaction in the performance of my task.

While I was thus engaged I observed a stranger coming up the lawn toward me. I bade him a very good morning, but he seemed disinclined to exchange civilities with me. He was a low-browed, roughish-looking fellow, and I conceived an immediate dislike for him.

"You 'll have to give me your name," said he, very gruffly.

"For what purpose?" I asked, for his tone and manner nettled me.

"I 'm a detective," said he, exhibiting a silver star on his vest front, "and I 'm on the trail of you ducks that sprinkle your lawns after legal hours. Oh, I 'm onto your racket."

"Sir," said I, indignantly, "I have made no racket. I am a quiet, law-abiding citizen, and this is my own lawn to do with as I please."

"Come, now," said he, insolently, "don't give me any funny business. You 're sprinklin' after hours and I 'm going to report you to police headquarters. There 's no use of kickin', so you 'd better give me your name an' save trouble."

"Sir," I cried, "Reuben Baker is not a name to be ashamed of, and if you think that by any of your underhand hocus pocus you can trespass on my premises and prevent my caring for my own property you are grandly mistaken."

"You 'll sing a different song to-morrer,"

said the fellow, and I am sure I heard him chuckling to himself as he walked away.

Later in the day I learned from neighbor Baylor that I had indeed transgressed the law by operating the lawn hose at ten o'clock in the morning. It seems that there is an ordinance imposing a fine upon all who sprinkle their lawns between eight o'clock in the morning and five o'clock in the afternoon.

I declared in very vigorous English that I would never submit to any such outrage, and my indignation touched the boiling point when, still later in the day, a policeman came to my house and handed me a document apprising me that I must give a good and sufficient bond for my appearance the next morning before his honor, Justice Fatty, to answer to the charge of having maliciously, etc., defied, disobeyed and broken the ordinance, etc. I went at once to seek the counsel of Lawyer Miles, for whose legal acumen and forensic eloquence I had harbored the profoundest veneration ever since I had heard his prosecution of a man named Tackleton for causing the death of neighbor Baylor's pet dog. I recall that on that occasion there was not a dry eye in the court and that even the defendant himself wept copiously; whereupon the presiding justice, fearing that he might be unduly influenced by the emotion of the auditors, ordered the constable to clear the room of everybody not a party to the cause. At this supreme moment Lawyer Miles, with streaming eyes and amid choking sobs, cried out: "Mercy, your honor; in the name of the tenderest and holiest of human considerations I appeal for mercy! Turn out the menfolks if you will, but spare, oh, spare the women and children."

Ever since this memorable occasion I have regarded Lawyer Miles as the foremost of living jurists, and it was the most natural thing in the world that I should determine to confide to him any legal business of mine that might arise — in which determination I was confirmed by a suspicion that Lawyer Miles never charged his neighbors any fee for his professional services.

I was not a little surprised when, having heard my story, Lawyer Miles counselled me to plead guilty to the charge and to pay the regulation fine, which together with the costs (so called), amounted to seven dollars and fifty cents. It was in vain that I represented to Lawyer Miles the outrage of punishing a man for seeking to beautify his premises, and thereby to contribute to the comfort and delectation of the public generally. Lawyer Miles took the narrow view that the ordinance had been violated, and that, therefore, the fine should be paid. "The ordinance may be an unwise one," said he. "In that event we should elect a city council that will repeal it. But so long as the law exists it should be enforced."

The advice of Lawyer Miles, coupled with the tears of Alice, finally prevailed. Alice fancied that I was in danger of being committed to prison, and she hysterically represented to me the horror of the ignominy which would ever thereafter attach to our family name. In one breath she proposed to send post haste for our pastor, the Rev. Dr. Sungaulus, in the hope that by means of his spiritual ministrations I might be dissuaded from further defiance of the law; in the next breath she conjured me by every regard I had for the future of our children — Galileo, Herschel, Fanny, Erasmus, and Josephine — to listen to the Voice of Reason. At the mention of Josephine's name I weakened, for, as I have already intimated to you, the innocent babe has acquired a powerful hold upon the tendrils of my heart. In an instant my anger departed.

"It shall be as you say, Alice : I will pay the fine and costs. But from this moment I consecrate my life to the election of councilmen from the Twenty-fifth Ward who will repeal that odious ordinance and make it legal for property-owners to sprinkle their lawns when and how they please."

In looking back over the short period of the history of "our house" I find no other incident so disagreeable as this one which I have just narrated. Even at this remote date I cannot refer to it without feeling my gorge rise. By nature I am peaceful, and I am exceeding slow to wrath. But anything that savors of injustice exasperates me to the degree of frenzy. I am still fixed in my determination to secure the repeal of the ordinance which robbed me of seven dollars and fifty cents and is jeoparding the lives of my lilac bushes, my peonies, my twin cherry-trees (George and Martha), and my grass. I intend to see that the matter is brought up at the next quarterly meeting of the Buena Park Benevolent and Protective Citizens' Association, and you can depend upon it that when that association speaks its tones are heard around the world and go thundering down the ages.

This affair of mine with the odious ordinance was duly reported in the daily newspapers through the delectable medium of the column headed "Minor Criminal Items." It did not conduce to my equanimity to see my name catalogued with persons arrested for sneak thievery, pocket-picking, drunkenness, brawling, and mayhem. I never before suspected that my friends made a practice of perusing the criminal calendar, but after the appearance of that disagreeable item in print I began to get letters from old acquaintances condoling with me and asking whether they could be of any service to me in my trouble. Some of these letters must have been dispatched in a spirit of humor, but I see nothing mirthfull in the association of an honest man's name with crime, and the people who have sought to poke fun at me in this unpleasant affair need not be at all surprised if I do not bow to them the next time we meet.

Another class of people I have no sympathy with are those who do not recognize in our purchase of a home a cause for genneral joy and congratulation. You may not believe it, but it is nevertheless a fact that within the last two months I have met people and apprised them of our purchase and they have never so much as expressed even the least bit of delight. My old friend Slashon Tomsing, who makes considerable pretense to being interested in the public welfare — why, when I met him at the Civic Federation rooms not long ago and began to tell him of our new home, instead of being swept away (as it were) upon a tidal wave of rapture, he immediately changed the theme of conversation and asked my opinion of bimetallism. I gave him to understand very distinctly that the public was in very

poor business if it suffered itself to become
interested in bimetallism or in any other ism
so long as it had an opportunity to discuss
"our new house" as a living, absorbing, and
burning theme.

Another friend, my old and particularly
valued friend, Professor Sniff, curator of Ma-
hon's Museum of Marvels—but I'll let that
affair pass; for Professor Sniff certainly did
not intend to wound my feelings by his apparent indifference; moreover, he has promised to send me for my private collection
all the duplicates that occur in section E of
his museum, which section is devoted exclusively to dried centipedes, tarantulas, and
beetles and to Mexican lizards in bottles of
alcohol.

All who have ever engaged in the enterprise of a new house will agree with me
when I say that nothing else wounds one
more deeply than the indifference of the rest
of humanity to what is nearest and dearest
to his heart.   When I walk the street nowadays I actually pity the crowds of people I
see, because, forsooth, they know nothing
of the great joy I have acquired in that

blessed house.   Alice made me take her to hear a Mme. Melba in Italian opera last month at the Auditorium.   As we came away Alice asked: " Was n't it grand ? "

" Yes," I answered, "and yet amid it all I was oppressed by a feeling of sadness. For, of all the six thousand souls in that splendid building, only you and I, dear Alice, were aware that the old Schmittheimer place had passed into the possession of the two happiest people on earth."

XV

THE QUESTION OF INSURANCE

MY neighbor, Mr. Teddy, called on me one morning as I sat under a willow tree watching the tinner at work on the roof and wondering whether it was really as nice and warm on a tin roof under an unobscured sun as it seemed to be.

"Do you know," said Mr. Teddy, cordially, "this is the first time I have ever visited this place. Frequently in my walks of an evening I have passed here, and, in common with others, I have admired the graceful slope of the lawn, the stately dignity of the trees, and the bright colors of the flowers that here and there dot the verdant expanse. Surely in the possession of this charming estate you are, my dear friend, one of the most fortunate of mortals. Your life amid these picturesque environments. in this sequestered spot, far from the din and turmoil of the urban throng, will be in every respect ideal — a dream, sir, a poetic dream."

You will perhaps understand by this time that I regard Mr. Teddy as an exceptionally worthy and pleasant gentleman.

"And," continued Mr. Teddy, "it would be cruel if your studious researches in this academic grove were by any chance to be interrupted by any harassing business care. The serpent of worldly solicitude, sir, should never be suffered to enter this veritable Eden."

"You are right, my good friend and neighbor," said I, "but how can I prevent the intrusion of care, since, alas! I am merely human?"

"It behooves you to make provision against every contingency," answered Mr. Teddy. "Do I understand that you carry insurance upon this residence?"

"Insurance? Why, no, I think not," said I. "Insurance is a matter I never thought of."

"Is it possible," cried Mr. Teddy, "that you have neglected to provide against that serious loss which would accrue if a careless workman were to drop a lighted match in yonder pile of shavings ? Think for one moment, sir, of the ruin that would confront you if this magnificent but uninsured architectural pile were to be swept away by the pale hand of the remorseless fire fiend! I beg of you to provide yourself with the means of redress ere you are overtaken by the bitter pill of adversity. Mr. Baker, your beautiful home should be insured at once!"

It then occurred to me for the first time that neighbor Teddy was the general western agent of the Royal Liliuokalani Fire, Marine and Accident Insurance Company of Hawaii. I have often wondered why a man when he embarks in the insurance business invariably attaches himself to a concern located in some far distant clime, and now that I am thinking of it, I will add that I have often wondered why the efficacy of patent medicines is so often testified to by the affidavits of people with strange names who reside in queer streets in obscure hamlets hundreds of miles distant from the place of publication.

"It would be wise of you," said Mr. Teddy, "to let me write you out a policy immediately. It is always prudent to take time by the forelock. Our rates are low, and, as you doubtless are aware, our company is the most prosperous in the world. We were awarded a medal at the World's Fair.

"I know absolutely nothing about these things," said I, candidly, " but I suppose we ought to have the place insured. I should be glad to have you drop around some evening and talk the matter over with Alice and me."

To this suggestion Mr. Teddy took very kindly and he promised to call very soon. As he retired down the gravel walk Colonel Bobbett Doller came up the same. The two gentlemen saluted each other very coldly.

"Colonel Doller is coming to talk to me about that twenty-five foot strip of land," says I to myself; but I was in error.

"Ah, good morning, neighbor Baker, good morning!" cried Colonel Doller, cheerily. "Beautiful weather we 're having — too dry, though, much too dry! All nature is parched. We need rain badly; otherwise the most lamentable consequences will follow. I dare say you have noticed by the paper how alarmingly prevalent conflagrations have become?"

"Have they?" I asked, in genuine surprise.

"Shockingly so," answered Colonel Doller. "The record is simply appalling. If this thing continues a lot of the little mushroom insurance companies will fail; it 's an ill wind that blows nobody good. The public will presently awaken to a realization of the danger of patronizing the irresponsible concerns which are trying to do business under the shadow of the old and reliable companies."

"Do you really think there will be a panic?" I asked.

"Among the small fry, yes," answered Colonel Doller; "but nothing short of a universal cataclysm will feaze to the slightest degree the Vesuvius Assurance Company (limited) of Piddleton, England, the oldest and staunchest insurance company in the world, of which I am, as perhaps you know, the general manager for the western hemisphere."

"We — and when I say we," continued Colonel Doller, "I mean the Vesuvius — we have a cash capital of eighteen million pounds, and a reserve fund of twelve million five hundred and sixty-eight thousand two hundred pounds, three shillings, and six pence. Our losses last year were six million three hundred thousand pounds in round numbers, and our premiums were eight million five hundred and sixty-three thousand two hundred and sixty-five pounds and eighteen pence. So you can see for yourself (for figures do not lie) that the Vesuvius is as solid as the everlasting hills."

"The Royal Liliuokalani is a pretty good company, is n't it?" says I.

"The Royal Liliuokalani?" repeated Colonel Doller. "The Royal Liliuokalani? Let me see — I don't know that I ever heard of it. It 's a Milwaukee concern, is n't it?"

"No," said I, "my understanding is that it is a Hawaiian enterprise."

"Possibly so — very likely it is," said Colonel Doller, indifferently. There are so many of these little schemes springing up nowadays that I do not pretend to keep track of them. If, however, you should at any time contemplate insuring you will, of course, come to the Vesuvius."

I repeated to Colonel Doller what I had told Mr. Teddy about the feasibility of consulting Alice. Colonel Doller replied that while the Vesuvius was entirely too big and too conservative a company ever to skirmish for business, he would, purely out of regard for his long friendship for me, call that evening to have a business talk with Alice and me.

Later in the day I had a visit from Frederick Jeems, another neighbor engaged in the profession of fire insurance. He began his attack adroitly by complimenting my new house and by regretting that I was shingling the roof.

"But so long as you 're insured," said he, carelessly, "I don't know that it makes any difference whether you use shingles or slate."

I confessed that I had not taken out any insurance, and this gave him the desired opportunity to bring up his batteries of eloquence, of argument, of statistics, and of

figures. Before he was done he had overwhelmed the Royal Liliuokalani of Hawaii
and the Vesuvius of Piddleton with a genuine avalanche of scorn and derision, and had
quite convinced me that the only solvent
and secure insurance concern in the world
was the Deutsche Kaiser of Bomberg-am-
Rhine. In an inspired moment I bade Mr.
Jeems come round that very evening to present his facts and figures to Alice, and I
laughed slyly to myself as I pictured the
meeting between himself, Mr. Teddy, and
Colonel Doller. This may strike you as
having been malicious, but I claim that under
the circumstances I was warranted in planning this practical joke.

Having disposed of these three gentlemen,
I flattered myself that I was temporarily done
with the vexatious details of insurance, and
I was getting ready to bank up one of the
flower beds with black dirt when who should
come along but another neighbor, and a very
charming one, too — Angus Cameron Macleod? For two years we have been more
or less intimate. Macleod combines many
strangely diverse accomplishments. He ex-

ecutes the sword dance with singular grace, and he recites Robert Burns' poems and passages from " Marmion " by the yard, and with inspiring animation. Although I am in no sense a music critic, nor even a connoisseur, I will confess that I have often been actually transported with delight by neighbor Macleod's rendition of " The Campbells Are Coming " on the bagpipes. At the same time he is a skilful rhetorician and severe logician, as all who have heard his defence of Presbyterianism will testify, and I will concede that I never heard anything more absorbingly fascinating than his exposition of the honest and ennobling old doctrine of infant damnation. If you knew Macleod you 'd agree with me that he is a man of parts.

" Now that your house is pretty nearly done," said Macleod, " you ought to take out some insurance in our company, the Bonny Thistle Marine of Inverness."

" But gracious me!" I cried in astonishment. " Why should I take out any marine insurance on a *house* ?"

" For the very best reason in the world,"

answered Mr. Macleod. "Your house stands within two hundred yards of one of the fiercest inland seas of the world. Even now you can hear the tempestuous billows dashing wildly upon yonder treacherous sands, and you can see the surf madly reaching out as if to overwhelm this fair spot with its fatal fury. At any time a tidal wave is likely to sweep in from the frowning shores of Michigan. Fancy for one moment what would become of this beautiful but delicate fabric if that mighty lake were to burst its confines and surge in one vast wall in this direction! Has not the immortal Scott truly said:

"Against the wrath of nature how vain
the works of man?

"My dear Baker, you certainly are too sensible a man to be blind to the security which is held out to you in this supreme moment of peril by the Bonny Thistle Marine of Inverness."

I admit that I knew not what to say. I had never before suspected any of these dangers which, according to my friends, now seemed imminent. On the one hand our cherished new house was threatened by fire; on the other hand that same dear edifice seemed to be doomed to a watery grave. Under these conflicting threatenings what was an inexperienced man to do? Heaven be praised, my presence of mind did not desert me. I referred Mr. Macleod to Alice, as I had referred the others. It was her house, and she would have to be responsible for it against the devouring elements.

That night I dreamed that the awful suggestions of Messrs. Teddy, Jeems, Doller, and Macleod had been realized. I dreamed that the new house was confronted upon one side by a wall of flame, and upon the other by a wall of water. Destruction and death seemed imminent. I dreamed that, trusting rather the mercy of the waves than the ferocity of the flames, I leaped into the billows and struggled like a Titan with them. I awoke, screaming with affright.

XVI

NEIGHBOR ROBBINS' PLATYPUS

I WISH you knew Burr Robbins. It is quite likely, however, that you *do* know him, for he has been conspicuously before the public for a number of years. Mr. Robbins lives just across the way from the old Schmittheimer place, and he has surrounded himself with comforts and luxuries of a most extraordinary character. He is a retired circus proprietor, and he has taken with him into retirement many of the most startling features of the menagerie which used to figure as one of the most delectable component parts of the "absolutely greatest agglomeration of marvels exhibiting under one canvas."

In his front yard Mr. Robbins pastures two trained buffalo, a sacred cow, a gnu (or horned horse), two musk deer, a giraffe, a woolly horse, a five-legged calf and a moose. In the back yard there are two white bear cubs, a baby elephant, a nest of pythons, half a dozen ostriches, a learned pig, several alligators and crocodiles, and a giant sloth from South America. The stable is well stocked with monkeys, parrots, eagles, lizards, tortoises and other curiosities, and in the watering trough are a sea serpent and a mermaid (said to be the only specimens of these marvels in a domesticated state).

Alice expressed some anxiety at first that the proximity of the strange creatures might prove unpleasant to us, and she strictly forbade little Erasmus associating with the pythons or pulling the crocodiles' tails. Mr. Robbins has assured us, however, that his pets are docile and trustworthy, and it is his custom to invite the little children of the neighborhood to visit and play with the most tractable of them.

I got acquainted with neighbor Robbins in a rather curious manner. His platypus escaped from its cage in the stable and sought refuge in our front yard. I discovered that it had made a nest in one of our lilac bushes and had laid an egg in it. With eggs at twenty cents a dozen and our family fond of custard, an industrious platypus is by no means an unwelcome visitor. When Mr. Robbins came looking for his vagrant pet I suggested that a flock of platypuses would be a decided improvement upon the poultry with which the average farmer stocks his farm. I was considerably surprised to learn from Mr. Robbins that the market price of platypuses is eight hundred dollars apiece, and I at once foresaw that this strange creature was not likely to become the dreaded competitor of the hen in the midst of us.

Erasmus and little Josephine became deeply interested in Mr. Robbins, and they are now spending a large share of their time in the society either of that fascinating gentleman or of his equally fascinating wild beasts. Erasmus has learned to throw a back-somersault with surprising ease and grace and to sing a comic song with electrical effect. These accomplishments he has acquired under the careful tutelage of Rufe Botts, formerly known to fame as Professor Botts, manager

of the Nonpareil Congress of Trained Dogs
and Trick Ponies. I understand that he also
served Mr. Robbins in "the palmy days " as
a clown in the ring during the regular performance and as a serio-comic vocalist at the
concert immediately after the show under
the great canvas. Relentless time, however,
rings in wondrous changes, and the whilom
Professor Rufus Botts, pride alike of the am-
phitheatre and of the concert stage, is now
plain Rufe Botts on a salary of four dollars a
week (and found) as Mr. Robbins' man of
all work.

Alice and I have feared that Rufe's influence
might not be beneficial to the children. It
pains us to observe that Josephine has
learned to ride a padded horse and to leap
with surprising certainty through a hoop and
over a banner. Erasmus does not disguise
his intention of joining a circus when he
reaches the age of maturity, and I happened
to overhear Rufe remark the other day that .
our daughter Fanny, with just a leetle more
practice, would make a ne plus ultra snake-
charmer and knife-thrower. Mr. Robbins
has laughed at our solicitude; he tells us that

these are the vagarious fancies and exuberant whims of youth and that they will duly die out. This is really very consoling to me, for I can conceive of nothing else more humiliating than the spectacle of our beloved Josephine flaunting around a circus ring upon the back of a fat horse and attired in shockingly scanty raiment. It would break his mother's heart if Erasmus were to diverge from that course in theology which she has mapped out and were to embark in the picturesque profession of turning somersaults in public. Our family reputation would surely be irreparably damaged if our Fanny were to be beguiled into the fascinating but hazardous arts of a snake-charmer and a knife-thrower! Heaven send that our fears be dissipated by future events!

And yet, full of temptations and of misery as I believe the career of a circus performer to be, I am entertained and instructed by neighbor Robbins' recital of his exploits and experiences, and I am deeply stirred by his narrative of the adventures he had in the capture of those same wild beasts which now embellish his expansive estate in Clarendon Avenue. Indeed, a peculiar interest is now attached by me to each particular beast, for I have heard Mr. Robbins tell how in their native jungles or on their native pampas or in their native lagoons or among their native rocky fastnesses he sought and found and comprehended the lemurs, the bisons, the alligators, the rackaboars, and the other marvels of zoölogy.

It is very pleasant, I can assure you, to listen to tales of adventure while one is engaged at the somewhat prosaic task of trimming a lilac bush or of weeding the pansy bed. Whenever he discovers me at this kind of toil neighbor Robbins comes over and leans up against a tree and beguiles the tedium of labor with a bit of personal experience. I can't begin to tell you how attached I have already become to Mr. Robbins. I have already made up my mind that when his own front lawn gets pretty well cleaned out I shall ask neighbor Robbins to pasture his sacred cow, horned horse, and five-legged calf in our front yard for a spell.

I shall never forget the shock I had one afternoon while Mr. Robbins and I were visiting on our front lawn. I had been pruning one of the poplars and Mr. Robbins was telling me of the difficulty Professor Rufus Botts and he had once had trying to teach the wild man of Borneo to eat olives and anchovy paste. Suddenly I saw a strange object pass up the street on a bicycle. I had never seen the like before. My acquaintance with Burr Robbins' menagerie had made me familiar with most of the curious forms of animal life, but never before had I seen so remarkable an object as I beheld upon that bicycle.

"Look there! Look quick!" said I to neighbor Robbins. "It is going up the street and it has wheels under it!"

"Where?" asked Mr. Robbins; "I don't see anything."

"Yes, you do," said I; "I mean the queer thing on the bicycle—can it be one of your trained animals that has got away?"

"Bless your soul, man," answered Mr. Robbins, "that 's not an animal! That 's a woman!"

"Oh, no, it is n't," said I. "No woman ever dressed like that."

"No woman ever dressed like that?" echoed Mr. Robbins, with a mocking laugh; "why, neighbor Baker, where have you been hiding so long that you 're so behind the times?"

"I 've not been hiding at all," said I, indignantly. "I 've been living in Evanston Avenue, and a very worthy locality it is, too!"

"And do you mean to tell me," asked Mr. Robbins, "that women don't ride the bicycle in Evanston Avenue?"

"Of course they do," said I, "but they don't look like *that!* The women that ride in Evanston Avenue wear dresses, the same as other women wear. This strange object (which you declare is a woman) wears pants!"

"Those ain't pants," said Mr. Robbins; "those are bloomers."

"I don't care what you call them," said I. "they 're pants just the same, and, what is more, very ill-fitting pants at that!"

"That," said Mr. Robbins, "is the new style of bicycle attire for the feminine sex. Shocking as it may appear to you, it is much more ample than the costume which I found to be popular among the female bicyclists of France during my visit to that country last summer."

"But you don't mean to tell me," said I, "that women make a practice of riding up and down Clarendon Avenue in pants!"

"Certainly, I do," said Mr. Robbins. "We do things in style over this way. Evanston Avenue is a century behind the times. Oh, you 'll learn a lot of things when you get moved over here into your new house."

"But I 'll not stand it!" I cried. "I 'll inform the police and I 'll have the law on these brazen creatures. What would Alice say! And what would become of Fanny and of little Josephine if they were brought up under the demoralizing influences of spectacles like that! Do you suppose I 'm going to have Galileo and Herschel corrupted? And little Erasmus — shall his pure, innocent mind be contaminated? Never, neighbor Robbins, never!"

But Mr. Robbins did not seem to view the matter at all as I did. It was evident that his long connection with the circus had calloused the sensibility of his perceptive faculties. He was inclined to jeer at what he termed my prudishness. I was glad to be back in Evanston Avenue once more, secure in an atmosphere of propriety. It was several hours, however, before I could get my mind away from thoughts of that woman in pants, so profoundly had her appearance in that strangely abbreviated costume shocked me.

XVII

OUR DEVICES FOR ECONOMIZING

UNLESS you want to render yourself liable to an attack of nervous prostration you should never watch a skilful workman nailing on lath. It is the most bewildering spectacle you can conceive of. I watched it for twenty minutes one day — it was when they were lathing the big front room downstairs, the library, and my brain began to reel as if I were intoxicated. I actually believe that if Uncle Si had not led me away and set me down under one of the willow-trees in the front yard I should have had a spell of sickness, and may be even now had been confined in the incurable ward of a lunatic asylum. I can't understand how they do it so accurately and so fast and with such apparent ease. The whole proceeding is so fascinating that I really believe that, next to proficiency in the science of astronomy, I should like to be an expert at nailing lath. In every line of mechanics my education has been grievously neglected.

Alice says that I am not practical enough to make a successful carpenter; she gets this unfair opinion of me from an incident in our early wedded life which she delights in recalling in the presence of people upon whom I am particularly desirous of making a favorable impression. It seems that when Galileo and Herschel were little tots I undertook to construct a playhouse for them in the back yard. This was at a time when I was exceptionally busied with my professional studies; Mars was rapidly approaching perihelion, and I had been commissioned by the Blue Island Society of the Arts and Sciences to prepare a chart of the bottle-neck seas. It would have been surprising indeed had I not been preoccupied — too absorbed in intellectual pursuits to cope successfully with any such worldly and prosaic thing as a playhouse in the back yard. Yet Alice insists that it is most amusing that I should have neglected to provide that structure with windows and a door, and that, as a natural consequence, I should have nailed myself up securely in that affair.

On another occasion I painted myself gradually into a corner while attempting to paint the floor of the spare chamber. Alice reproached me bitterly for this; she said she supposed everybody knew that a floor should always be painted toward, and not away from the door. Alice seems never to consider that few other people are gifted with such intuitions as she has, but are compelled to drag along through life learning by experience.

I do not wish to be understood as complaining or railing against fate because I am not skilled in mechanics; I recognize as a distinct boon the fact that I am awkward in the use of tools, and the further fact that I have no ambition in the direction of mechanical endeavor has doubtless saved me many a bruised thumb and a vast amount of hard labor. When I see my neighbors tinkering away at their storm windows and garbage boxes and grape vine trellises and dog kennels and window screens and front gates, I do not neglect to thank heaven that Alice has the best of reasons for not asking me to engage in similar odd jobs about our house.

Still, I am sure that, if I ever *do* engage in any avocation, it will be that of nailing lath, an employment requiring an exercise of patience, of intelligence, and of skill to the highest degree.

Until we bought the new place I had no idea that the expense of conducting an establishment of one's own was so large. It seems, however, that when one has once become a property-owner there is no end to the things one must have and cannot get along without. It is impossible to say how or where the venders of patent arrangements find out about you, but no sooner do you buy a place of your own than you are run to death by people who actually prove to you that you *must* have what they have to sell.

Alice and I are very happy in the confidence that we have secured a simple device which is going to reduce our coal bill by at least fifty per cent.; it is a fuel-saving machine which is to be attached to our new steam-heating apparatus, and if it accomplishes anything like what the agent said it would, why, it is worth five dollars ten times over! And we are expecting wonders, too, of the gas-saving apparatus for which we have paid three dollars and which is to be attached to the meter with such pleasing results that we shall have five times more light at a saving of at least sixty per cent in cost.

I find upon consulting my expense account for May that during that month alone Alice and I purchased no fewer than thirty devices of an economical character. We have three different kinds of smoke-consumers, an automatic carpet-sweeper, a bottle of lightning polish for plate-glass, a dish-washing machine, a knife-scourer, a potato-parer, two automatic lawn-hose reels, a sewer-gas consumer, a patent ashes-sifter, etc., etc. It has required a considerable outlay of money to get stocked up with these things, but we regard them as a very wise investment. It is wholly consistent with our policy of economy to provide ourselves with the means of making a marked reduction in our expenses. We flatter ourselves that before we have been in our house six months we shall have demonstrated that we are not upon earth for the purpose of enriching gas companies and other soulless corporations.

But I think the wisest investment we have made is the insurance policy which we have taken out on Alice's life. The incident came about so curiously that I feel inclined to tell it in detail. I was one evening sitting out in front of our house—the rented one, I mean—watching the stars gradually making their appearance in the cerulean vault, and I was marvelling at the endless wonders of the heavenly expanse, when I became aware that somebody was approaching. I saw that this somebody was my Sheridan Road friend and neighbor, Treese Smith. He was whistling softly to himself an air which I did not recognize, but which my daughter Fanny (who is a music connoisseur) identified as "My Pearl Is a Bowery Girl." Presuming that he was coming to pay me a neighborly call, I arose to meet him. Fancy my amazement when upon beholding me Mr. Smith burst into tears. I do not remember ever to have been more astounded than by this sudden transition from gayety to grief. I could hardly find words to ask my friend what trouble had befallen him.

"I was hoping to meet no one," he sobbed, "for I am in no condition of mind to associate with my fellow-beings."

"It is evident," I interposed, "that some great sorrow has come upon you; surely you would not hesitate to come to me for sympathy."

"You are right," said Mr. Smith, making a heroic effort to gather himself together. "It would be selfish of me not to give so dear a neighbor as you a chance to share my misery. Read this."

He handed me a bit of printed stuff which he had evidently cut from a newspaper. I stood under the street lamp and read it in this wise:

KANSAS CITY, May 23.— During the thunder-storm to-day Mrs. Bolivar Bowers, wife of the well-known scientist, was struck and destroyed by lightning. Deceased leaves a husband and five children; no insurance.

"Ah, I see," said I in my gentlest tone;

"she was a dear friend—perhaps a relative of yours."

"No, not that," said Mr. Smith, still sobbing; "you misinterpret my grief. This party was in no way akin to me except under that common descent from the old Adam which makes all humanity brothers and sisters. I did not know deceased, nor did I ever see her."

"Then why," I asked, in some astonishment, "why are you so moved by the news of her death ?"

"To one of my nature," exclaimed Mr. Smith, "the circumstances detailed in this item are most painful to contemplate. We find here recorded the sudden demise of the sole support of a husband and five children —a wife and mother snatched away by death, leaving a helpless family without any visible means of support."

"But why without any means of support ?" I asked.

"It says so," answered Mr. Smith. "The husband is a scientist and is therefore by nature and by occupation disqualified for earning a livelihood."

"Surely enough," said I, "that is quite true."

"Can you picture a more distressing scene," continued Mr. Smith, still in tears, "than that of this helpless father and his five little ones standing above that lifeless lady and wondering where their food and raiment will come from now? It is sad, it is agonizing, it is awful! And yet it all might have been averted — all this solicitude about the future. Had Mrs. Bolivar Bowers taken out a policy in my company, the International Mutual Tontine Life Insurance Company of Paw Paw, Indiana, the aspect to-day would have been different, and Bolivar Bowers and his callow brood of little Bowerses would have reason to bless the rod that smote them. Ah, friend Baker, the International Mutual Tontine has done a glorious work toward mitigating the wrath of the grim destroyer; under the grace of its soothing balm bereavement becomes an actual pleasure, death loses its sting, and the grave its victory."

From this small, casual beginning followed that train of explanation and argument upon

Mr. Smith's part which led to Alice's taking out a life policy in the Indiana company. Mr. Smith is a man of broad and deep human sympathies. Had he not happened upon that newspaper item, had his heart not gone out in passionate sympathy toward the bereaved Bolivar Bowers and his little ones, had he not wandered in an irresponsible paroxysm of grief in the direction of my house that evening, and had he not confided his sorrow to me — why, then we should not have known of the greatest of human benefactors, and Alice would not now be safe (so to speak) in the bosom of the International Mutual Tontine Life Insurance Company of Paw Paw.

I do not regard these things as accidental; they are special providences.

XVIII

I STATE MY VIEWS ON TAXATION

O F the many friends who hastened to congratulate us when they heard that we had acquired a home, none was more delighted than Gamlin Harland. I take it for granted that you have read Mr. Harland's numerous books, and that you know all about Mr. Harland himself. Not to know of him is to argue one's self unknown.

My first meeting with Mr. Harland was at a single-tax convention six years ago; he was a delegate to that convention from Wisconsin, and I was a delegate from Illinois. I was a delegate because the manager of the party, who lives in New York, could n't find anybody else to serve as the delegate from the congressional district in which I lived. I thought that rather than have that district unrepresented I ought to serve, and so I did.

The acquaintance I then made with Gamlin Harland soon ripened into friendship, and this intimacy has lasted ever since. Mr. Harland insists that I am a single-tax man, and it may be that I am in theory, although I certainly am not in practice; for I never have paid any tax of any kind, be it single or double.

As soon as he heard of our purchase Mr. Harland came out to inspect the premises, and of course he was delighted.

" This will make a new man of you," said he to me. " It will take your mind off your impracticable star-gazing and moonshining, and divert your attention into the channels of realism. These premises are so spacious as to admit of your engaging to a considerable extent in agriculture; you can now lay aside the telescope and the spectrum for the spade and the hoe; the field of speculation can be abandoned for this noble acre which I hope soon to see smiling into an abundant harvest."

"Yes," said I, "it is my purpose to engage largely in the cultivation of flowers."

"Pshaw!" cried Mr. Harland, "there you

go again! Don't you know that flowers are wholly worthless except in so far as they pander to the gratification of a sensuous appetite? It would be a crime to surrender these opportunities to ignoble uses. You must raise vegetables here, or perhaps some of the small fruits would thrive better in this rich sandy soil."

Investigation satisfied Mr. Harland that blackberries were *the* particular kind of small fruit to which the soil seemed adapted. I was not surprised at this, for I knew that the blackberry was a favorite with Mr. Harland — in fact, Mr. Harland is the only author I know of who has written a novel whose plot hinges (so to speak) upon a blackberry. So passionately fond of this fruit is he that he devotes a part of the year to cultivating blackberries on his Wisconsin farm. There are invidious persons who intimate that his only reason for cultivating the blackberry is to be found in the fact that nothing else will grow on his farm, and presumably you have heard the epigram which the romanticists have perpetrated at Mr. Harland's expense, and which represents that ambitious and aggressive gentleman as raising blackberries in summer and —— in winter.

After getting me thorougly inoculated with the blackberry idea, and having duly impressed me with his theory that true manhood consisted of making one's self unspeakably miserable and sweaty with a shovel and a hoe, Mr. Harland broached his favorite topic, and ventured the assertion that now that I was the possessor of taxable property I would become as rabid a single-tax advocate as Henry George himself. I answered that I already advocated a single-tax system, for the reason that if we could only once get a single-tax system in vogue we should then be but one remove from no taxation at all, and would have less difficulty in securing that desirable end ultimately.

The truth of the matter is, I object to taxation only in so far as it affects me. I have no objection to other folk being taxed, but I do not fancy being taxed myself. I agree with Brother Harland that there is palpable injustice in making an industrious and public-spirited man pay for the so-called privilege of building himself a home; he pays the carpenters and masons and painters for making that home, and he is then expected to pay the city and the State for having invested his hard earnings in a permanent enterprise which gives employment to the laborer, which beautifies the neighborhood, and which enhances the value of the adjacent property. The object of taxation (as Mr. Harland asserts and as I believe) is to enrich the office-holding class, a class of loose morality, utterly heartless and utterly conscienceless, and I agree with Mr. Harland in the opinion that the time is not far distant when the honest people of this country will arise as one man and subvert the corrupt hand of politics which is now grinding us under the iron heel of oppression.

It is seldom that I give expression to my views upon this subject, for the reason that I fear they may be misinterpreted. I have always had an apprehension that I would be mistaken for an anarchist, which I am not; I am an advocate of peace and of the laws; I do not believe in violence of any kind.

And now that I am speaking of violence, I am reminded of an incident which illustrates

the thoughtless cruelty of too many of our
youth. It was scarcely two weeks ago that
I detected a boy (apparently about twelve
years of age) climbing one of the willow trees
in our old Schmittheimer place. I crept up
on him unawares and speedily became satisfied that he was after the eggs in a bird's
nest that nestled cozily in a crotch of the
limbs. I shouted lustily at the young scape-
grace, and his confusion convinced me that
my suspicions were correct. I kept him in
his uncomfortable position in the tree until
I had lectured him severely for the cruelty he
contemplated and until I had exacted from
him a promise that he would forever thereafter abstain from the practice of robbing
birds' nests. The tears which trickled down
his face assured me no less than his solemn
protests did that the lad was indeed penitent,
but the fellow had no sooner descended from
the tree and reached a point of safety the other
side of the fence than he gave utterance to sentiments which wholly disabused my mind of
all faith in his previous professions of reform.

I have never been able to understand what
pleasure can accrue from the spoliation of the

homes of birds, the beautiful musical creatures
that contribute so largely toward making the
world cheerful. One of the pleasantest re-
collections of my boyhood is that in all that
active period I never once killed or wounded
a bird or robbed its nest. And I think that
the kindest act I ever did — at least the one
which I recall with the most satisfaction —
was my release of a caged bird. A careless,
heedless neighbor had caught and caged a
redbird, and the mournful twittering of the
poor creature as he fluttered incessantly behind the bars of his prison pained and
haunted me. The redbird can never be rec-
onciled to confinement; he is of the forest;
the wildness of his peculiar note indicates
the restlessness of his nature. So for nearly
a year the melancholy twittering and the
fluttering of that caged bird haunted me.

One morning — it was in the gracious May
time — I awoke early. The sun was just
coming up and was kissing the tears from
lovely Nature's face. The air was full of
coolness and of sweet smells. Then, hearing the querulous note of the imprisoned
bird upon the porch yonder, I determined to

set the poor thing free. So I dressed myself
and stole out into the graciousness of the
early morning. To my last day I shall not
forget the delight, the rapture, with which
that released bird mounted from the door-
way of his cage and sped away!

One of the most treasured relics I have is
a poem which my father wrote when I was
a little boy. My father was a native of Maine,
but for all that he was a man of sentiment
and he had much literary taste, and ability,
too. The poem which he gave me, and
which I have always treasured, will (if I am
not grievously in error) touch a responsive
chord in many a human heart, for all humanity looks back with tenderness to the time
of youth.

THE MORNING BIRD

A bird sat in the maple tree
And this was the song he sang to me:
" O little boy, awake, arise!
The sun is high in the morning skies;
The brook's a-play in the pasture lot
    And wondereth that the little boy
It loveth dearly cometh not
    To share its turbulence and joy;

The grass hath kisses cool and sweet
For truant little brown bare feet —
So come, O child, awake, arise !
The sun is high in the morning skies ! "

So from the yonder maple tree
The bird kept singing unto me ;
But that was very long ago —
I did not think — I did not know —
Else would I not have longer slept
   And dreamt the precious hours away ;
Else would I from my bed have leapt
   To greet another happy day —
A day, untouched of care and ruth,
With sweet companionship of youth —
The dear old friends which you and I
Knew in the happy years gone by !

Still in the maple can be heard
The music of the morning bird,
And still the song is of the day
That runneth o'er with childish play ;
Still of each pleasant old-time place
   And of the old-time friends I knew —
The pool where hid the furtive dace,
   The lot the brook went scampering through ;
The mill, the lane, the bellflower tree
That used to love to shelter me —
And all those others I knew *then*,
But which I cannot know again !

Alas ! from yonder maple tree
The morning bird sings not to me ;
Else would his ghostly voice prolong
An evening, not a morning, song
And he would tell of each dear spot
   I knew so well and cherished then,
As all forgetting, not forgot
   By him who would be young again !
O child, the voice from yonder tree
Calleth to *you*, and not to *me* ;
So wake and know those friendships all
I would to God I could recall !

XIX

OTHER PEOPLE'S DOGS

WHEN I discovered one morning that my young sunflowers and my tomato vines had been cut down during the night by some lawless depredator I was mightily incensed. I had not supposed that there was anybody so mean as to commit such a wanton destruction. The value of the property destroyed was not large; I had paid but five cents apiece for the twenty tomato vines, and the young sunflowers were a present from Fadda Pierce. The intrinsic value of these things was so small as to cut no figure in my mind, but having watched the graceful creatures wax large and comely from mere sprouts it was quite natural that I should have a strong sentimental attachment for them. For the fruit of the tomato vine I care nothing, but I had with much satisfaction pictured the enjoyment which Alice and the children would derive from the luscious tomatoes which I flattered myself were to ripen upon our own vines under the genial August sun.

Moreover, I had already made up a list of the names of city friends to whom I intended to send handsome specimens of these first fruits of my experiments in farming; the Reillys, the Lynches, the Chapins, the Maxwells, the Scotts, the Fayes, the Deweys, the Morrises, the Millards, the Larneds, the Fletchers, the Ways — these and other fortutunate cronies were to be made recipients of my bounty in case the fruit held out. I will say nothing of the pleasing future I depicted for the sunflowers; the sunflower is a particular favorite of mine, presumably because it is one of the very few flowers I am capable of identifying.

My impulse, when beholding the tomato vines and sunflowers cut down in the innocence of youth, was to determine not to pursue gardening further. To this mood succeeded a fit of anger, and I was so outraged by the destruction I beheld that I would cheerfully have given any sum of money I could have borrowed of my neighbors for information leading to the apprehension of the perpetrator of this brutal wrong.

As it was, I wrote out an offer of five dollars reward upon a sheet of letter paper and nailed it with four large wire nails to a maple tree in front of the place, where all passers-by could see and read it. Later in the day I went to tell Fadda Pierce of the trouble which had befallen me, and he consoled me with the assurance that the work of destruction had been wrought — not by a human being, as I had surmised, but by cutworms, a kind of reptile that plies its nefarious trade between two days for no other apparent purpose than that of making gentlemen farmers like myself miserable.

Fadda Pierce told me that Paris green was an effective antidote against these destructive worms, and I have ordered a barrel of it from the city. I intend to spread a layer of this Paris green over all our flower and vegetable beds; the contrast thus presented to the dull, sere brown of our lawn will be very pleasing to the eye. In fact, I am not sure that it would not be cheaper to color our whole lawn with Paris green than to attempt to revive it with water, which can be used with legal liberality only between the first of November and the first of May.

By way of illustrating what a mockery our national Department of Agriculture is, I will say that I wrote to Secretaty Morton about the cutworms and asked that he suggest an antidote against the same. Although five weeks have elapsed since I dispatched that letter I have had no word of any kind from the Department of Agriculture. I feel the slight all the more keenly because I am a personal acquaintance of Secretary Morton's, having been introduced to and shaken hands with him at the quadrennial convention of the Western Academy of Science at Omaha in 1884. Prompt attention to my letter was due on the score of old friendship. The Secretary of Agriculture will recognize his error in offending me if ever he becomes a candidate for the presidency. Reuben Baker never forgets an affront.

But, though my sunflowers and my tomato vines suffered as I have narrated, my potatoes were doing finely. The potato patch is located in the back yard, near the poplar trees; it is in the shape of the Big Dipper, and I took the precaution to plant the potatoes in the new of the moon. The first planting never amounted to anything, for the reason that I peeled them and cut out the eyes before putting them in their hills. I learned subsequently that this was as fatal a course as it were possible to pursue. You must never peel potatoes or cut out their eyes if you want them to grow. I do not know why this is so, but it is. At any rate, the second crop I planted was a success. Every day I dug down into the hills to see how the potatoes were progressing, and I was thus enabled to keep track of the development of the tender fruit.

My young friend Budd Taylor provided me with a dozen ears of seed popcorn which I planted in a warm, bright spot and which soon bristled up in splendid style. I think it likely that, but for the birds, I should have had a crop of popcorn sufficient to supply the Chicago market, for I never before saw anything like that corn for luxuriance and thrift. How the birds ever found out about it will doubtless remain a mystery.

The birds I refer to proved to be blackbirds, although for a time I mistook them for young crows. One morning I detected about three dozen of the poaching rogues stalking through the grass in the direction of my corn-patch, and, almost before I knew it, the feathered rascals had played havoc with my promising crop of popcorn. Then I remembered that I had read and seen pictures in books of scarecrows; so I dressed up a figure and set it up near the corn patch. It was really a very good counterfeit of a man, as indeed it ought to have been, for the clothing I used was far from ragged, and Alice had been intending to send it to a poor relative of hers in Nebraska.

The night after I had set up this lay figure in the yard a policeman came along Clarendon Avenue for the first time in his professional career. He espied the figure in the yard and at once mistook it for a thief who had come to steal our lawn hose. With a gallantry and with a devotion to duty which cannot be too highly commended, the in-

trepid policeman opened fire with his revolver and put seven holes through the
scarecrow before he discovered his mistake.

The cannonading awakened Major Ryson,
one of the nearest neighbors, and that discreet gentleman immediately set his bull terrier loose. This sagacious but vindictive
animal bore down upon the scene of action
and treed the policeman the first thing.
Having expended all his ammunition upon
the lay figure, the policeman had no means of
interchanging compliments with his assailant,
and was therefore compelled to spend the
night in a willow. Meanwhile the bull terrier encountered the scarecrow, and, mis-
taking it for a human being, soon tore that
unfortunate object into ten thousand pieces.
Next day our lawn was literally strewn with
straw and buttons and remnants of what
had once been a very decent suit of clothes.

This reference to Major Ryson's bull terrier
reminds me of the visit which the Baylors' dog
paid to our new premises. The Baylors' dog
is a St. Bernard about a year old and weighing one hundred and seventy-five pounds.
Most of the time this amiable leviathan is

confined in the Baylors' back yard, a spot hardly large enough to admit of the leviathan's turning around in it. The evening to which I refer the Baylors made a pilgrimage to our new house for the purpose of ascertaining whether we had put in a copper kitchen sink or a galvanized iron one. I can't imagine what possessed them to do it, but they took the St. Bernard with them. The sense of freedom which this playful beast felt upon being let loose in our extensive yard proved wholly uncontrollable, and while the Baylors were investigating the sink question the amiable leviathan gallivanted about the premises with that elephantine exuberance which is to be expected of a St. Bernard one year old and weighing one hundred and seventy-five pounds. Adah (who has an eye to the beautiful) had planted a vast number of nasturtiums and red geraniums, and under one of the oak trees had trained numerous graceful, dainty vines, which, as I recall, are known to horticultural amateurs as 'cobies.

In the twinkling of an eye the Baylor leviathan swept these blossoming innocents

out of existence, and in other twinklings he
wrought desolation among the peonies, the
pansies, and other floral objects upon which
the women folk had lavished a wealth of patient care. A bull in a china-shop could
hardly create the havoc which the Baylor
pup, with his one hundred and seventy-five
pounds of animal spirits, wrought in our
lawn. Next morning the lawn looked as
if it had been honored with a nocturnal visi-
tation from Burr Robbins' galaxy of domesticated wild beasts.

Curiously enough, the Baylors thought it
was very funny. I don't know why it is,
but it can't be denied that it *is* a fact that those
acts which in other people's pups strike us
as strangely improper, become in our own
pups the most natural and most mirth-pro-
voking performances in the world. I recall
the anger with which neighbor Baylor drove
neighbor Macleod's mastiff off his porch one
evening because that mastiff attempted to
make his way through the screen door behind which the family cat was visible. In
this instance the Macleod mastiff was simply
following the predominating instinct of the

canine kind, and neighbor Baylor hated the
unreasonable beast for it. Yet I 'll warrant
me that while his own lubberly pup was
prancing around over our flower beds neighbor Baylor regarded the performance as the
most cunning and most charming divertise-
ment in the world.

It is much the same way with children.
If I were put upon oath, I should have to admit that the very same antics which I regard
as most seemly (not to say fascinating) in my
own pretty little darlings I do not approve
of at all when I see them attempted by the
awkward, homely children of my neighbors.

XX

I ACQUIRE POISON AND EXPERIENCE

THERE is no telling to what unparalleled extent I should have carried my agricultural work but for a happening which interrupted my career in that direction and temporarily invalidated me for the performance of all manual labor. To make short of a long and painful story, I will tell you at once that in the very midst of my agricultural triumphs I was rudely awakened to a realization of the fact that I had been badly poisoned by ivy. The luxuriant growth in one part of our lawn which in my innocence I had mistaken for infant oak trees and had nurtured with great assiduity proved to be the poison vine which is shunned alike of knowing man and beast.

The truth about this insiduous plant was not revealed to me until after the harm was done. I awoke one night to find my hands and wrists afflicted with so pestiferous an itching that it verily seemed to me as if the points of ten thousand thousand hot needles were being thrust into my cuticle. There are no words capable of expressing how torturesome this affliction is; to my physical suffering there was added a distinct mental disquietude arising from a sense of injustice that nature, supposed to be so benignant to her friends, should have punished me so grievously for having sought to cultivate and foster her arts.

I was shocked, too, to discover that my misfortune awakened no feeling of sympathy in others; nay, my neighbors seemed to regard it rather as a joke that I, a scientist of no mean ability (if I *do* say it myself), should have fallen victim to the commonest and most vicious of all destroyers of human happiness. The amount of badinage, sarcasm, and irony indulged in by these unfeeling folk at the expense of "Farmer" Baker (as they now jocosely dubbed me) would fill a royal octavo volume. I assure you that I regarded this species of humor as impertinent to the degree of atrocity.

My family physician, Dr. Hodges, prescribed several vials of pellets which bore a striking resemblance to one another, but whose virtues I was solemnly assured depended wholly upon my strict observance of the *ordo* of their administration internally, which *ordo* may have been simple and clear enough to Dr. Hodges, but was to me as intricate and complicated as a Bradshaw railway guide. Furthermore, having ascertained by artful inquiry what viands and beverages I particularly liked, Dr. Hodges strictly forbade my indulgence in them, and such articles of food and drink as I was particularly averse to he recommended for my diet.

Meanwhile I was meeting constantly with people who had been afflicted with ivy poisoning, and these kind, cheery souls encouraged me with recitals of their experiences. I was told that it took seven years for ivy poison to get out of the system; that every year during the ivy season (whatever that may mean) there would be a recurrence of this pestiferous eruption, sometimes in one part of the body, sometimes in another, and not unfrequently upon the whole surface. There were, of course, numerous nostrums warranted to allay the fiery tingling and maddening stinging of the malady, and, as I cheerfully adopted every suggestion that came to my ears, I was presently stocked up with enough salves and solutions to fill an apothecary-shop, and my associates began to complain that I was as redolent of odors as a chemical laboratory. Naturally enough, therefore, I became morbid and despondent, and began to regard myself as a mercilessly afflicted and shunned thing.

But amid all this trouble there came to me one big, bright ray of satisfaction. I remembered that, when Alice took out a life policy with neighbor Treese Smith, I also took out an accident policy with the same gentleman in the Wabash Mutual Internecine Association of Indiana. There was, as you can well understand, a heap of consolation in the thought that no matter how little or how much or how long I suffered, the Wabash concern would have to pay for it. As I recollected, the insurance was fifty dollars a week during incapacity for work. If, therefore, the ivy poison remained in my system seven years, the amount of insurance due me would be—let me see:

Seven years — three hundred and sixty-four weeks.

Three hundred and sixty-four weeks at fifty dollars per week — eighteen thousand two hundred dollars.

This was, indeed, a considerable sum of money! I began to understand that, viewed from a purely business standpoint, my affliction might become financially profitable. It even occurred to me that in case the Wabash company paid promptly, and I got used to the tearing ebullitions of the ivy poison, I might contrive to get a renewal of the malady at the end of the first seven years. I wondered that, with this opportunity of getting rich cum otio et cum dignitate, there were so many poor people in the world; however, I mentally resolved not to discover my shrewd plan to anybody else.

When I called upon neighbor Treese Smith I was prudent enough to let him know that I probably had the worst case of ivy poisoning ever heard of, and with more than common pride I exhibited to him my hands and wrists in confirmation of my claims. Mr. Smith (whom you already know as a man of tender feelings and broad sympathies) expressed himself as being very sorry for me, and he asked me if I had tried certain remedies, which he named.

As it was another kind of remedy I was after, I adroitly led the conversation up to the proper point, and then I intimated that it would not harrow up my feelings if I were tendered a payment on account of my accident policy in the Wabash Mutual Internecine Association of Indiana. I liked Smith, and I felt that I ought to be candid with him. I told him that it was pretty generally agreed by the medical profession that when a person once got a dose of poison ivy it remained in his system for seven years, during which period it worked its baleful offices off and on with varying malignance. I recognized the fact that I had a valid claim on the Wabash company for fifty dollars a week for seven years; that the total amount of money due or paid me by said company at the end of the natural life of the ivy poison would be a trifle over eighteen thousand dollars. I told Mr.

Smith that I was not disposed to take advantage of or to be too hard on the Wabash company, and that, being naturally of a conservative disposition, I was willing to compromise this matter for — say — well — ten thousand dollars, and cancel the policy.

Mr. Smith answered me in the tone and with the manner of one who is seeking to break bad news gradually and gently to another.

" It is painfully clear to me," said the kind, sympathetic man, "that you have not read the conditions upon which your accident policy is issued to you. I fear that when you come to examine it more carefully you will learn that in this case you have no claims upon our company — or, perhaps, I should say *the* company, since I am merely its agent and have nothing to do with the framing of its contracts."

"I have the instrument with me," said I, producing the policy. "I have read it carefully and understand it fully. It is a simple, short, straightforward document, and the type is so big and clear that even a child could read it."

"Alas," said Mr. Smith, with a sigh, "I fear you have not read the conditions; you will find them on the other side of the sheet, printed in small type."

I turned the page, and surely enough there were a number of paragraphs under the title of "The Conditions"; they were printed in small type and pale-blue ink.

"But what have 'conditions' to do with this case?" I asked. "I got insured in the Wabash Mutual Internecine company against accident, and here I've had an accident! Ivy poison is as severe an accident as can happen to any animal, except, perhaps, an alligator or a rhinoceros, and I think I'm entitled to my money."

"You are quite right from your standpoint," said Mr. Smith, "but it is not the correct standpoint. You are insured (as you will see by referring to your policy) as an A No. 1 risk. Turn to the conditions, and you will observe that our A No. 1 risks are insured against accident by lightning only. If, now, you had been struck by lightning instead of by ivy, and if the subtle electric fluid had impaired your physical economy, or imparted to your veins any noxious rheum or any venom wherefrom either temporary or permanent harm or disquietude accrued to you, then you would have a legal and just claim against our — I mean *the* company."

"But I supposed I was insured against every kind of accident," said I. "When it comes to getting pay for an accident, a dislocation of a toe is quite as desirable, in my opinion, as a broken neck."

"Ah, but insurance companies must differentiate," said Mr. Smith. "There are so many kinds of accidents that it is absolutely necessary to have grades and classes and differences and distinctions. You are insured against lightning: you belong to A No. 1. If you were insured against a broken leg you would be in X No. 2, or against a sprained wrist in H No. 3. My recollection is that our policies of insurance against poison ivy are written in Q No. 4, but I am not positive. If, however, you care to profit by this annoying experience and desire to insure against ivy poison, I will look the matter up the first thing to-morrow and write you out a policy at once. In your case the policy should be made out for a period of fourteen years, since your present dose of poison will not lose its efficacy for seven years, and that will render insurance taken *after the fact* inoperative."

There was a heavy thunder shower the next day, and I stood out in it all the time in the hope of getting a chance to claim remuneration from the Wabash Mutual Internecine Association. But the lightning dodged me as if I had been a sacred and charmed object. I made up my mind that it was folly to try to get even with the insurance concern, and since a farming career was now closed against me, I determined to devote my spare time to watching the progress of affairs inside our new house and to coöperate with Alice and Adah and our feminine neighbors in their herculean task of "having things as they should be."

XXI

WITH PLUMBERS AND PAINTERS

IT did not take me long to find out that, in the treatment of the interior of the new house, Alice had fallen a victim to the influence of the Denslow-Baylor-Maria schools. I was not much surprised by this discovery, for I had known for some time that Alice regarded the Denslows and the Baylors as people of rare taste, and it was quite natural (as every unprejudiced person will allow) that, associating with Adah continually and being bound to her by ties of consanguinity, Alice should be susceptible to Adah's hortations, incitements, impulsations, and instigations.

At any rate, I found that our new house was to be a conspicuous intermingling and interblending of the Denslow, Baylor, and Maria styles of architecture. The big front room downstairs, the library, was distinctly Denslowish, and so was the big front room up-stairs, as well as the butler's pantry and the reception-room. The Baylor influence manifested itself in the spare bedroom and the dining-room, and the Maria influence (thanks to Adah) was clearly exhibited in the front and side porches, in my bedroom, and in the several hallways. Alice insisted that the house was to be strictly old colonial and also requested me to speak of it as such in the presence of visitors, particulary in the hearing of her relatives from the country when they came into the city next September to do their winter buying.

In my fancy I can already picture the dear girl putting on airs with those guileless rural folk who know no more about the architectural and the decorative arts than an unclouted Patagonian knows of the four houses of the Jesuitical order. Nor do I know much about those things, and I am glad that I do not, for if I had devoted my early years of study to plinths, architraves, columns, dados, friezes, pediments, sconces, wainscots, cornices, capitals, entablatures, and such like, how could I have originated my theory of star-drift and how would humanity have been enlightened upon the all-important subjects of the asteroids, the satellites of the star Gamma in Scorpio, the atmosphere on the other side of the moon, the depth of the Martian bottle-neck seas, the probability of the existence of natural gas wells in Jupiter, etc., etc.? If I had been a Linnæus or a Buffon instead of Reuben Baker, I should have never suffered myself to fall an innocent victim to poison ivy — yes, that is true, but at the same time my now famous theory of double stars and my equally famous theory as to the several elements in comets' tails would have been denied to the world. No one man can combine within himself all human genius; in all modesty I declare myself satisfied with being simply Reuben Baker.

While I devoted my attention to out-of-door affairs — by which I mean care of the lawn, of the flower-beds, and of the vegetable patches — I had a comparatively tranquil existence. Having transferred the base of my operations (or perhaps I should say my observations) indoors, I found numerous disagreements and misunderstandings to distract me. I was not long in finding out that there were two factions (so to speak) in charge of the department of the interior. Parties of the first part were Alice and all our feminine neighbors; party of the second part was Uncle Si.

You see, there had never been anything more explicit than a verbal understanding between Uncle Si and Alice; the two had talked the matter all over at the start, and they agreed upon every theory so nicely that I do not wonder they decided that a written contract was not necessary. Uncle Si did some figuring which resulted in his saying that he would reconstruct the old house and build an addition for the even sum of two thousand dollars. Very few specifications were made, but there was a pretty clear verbal understanding reached, and the consequence was as distinct a misunderstanding as the work progressed. Most of the trouble was over the detail of hardwood. Alice was sure that Uncle Si had agreed to put in hardwood floors and trimmings throughout; Uncle Si expostulated that he had never thought of so preposterous a project, since it would have bankrupted him as sure as his name was Silas Plum.

The result was that Alice never went near the new house that she did not groan and moan and declare that Georgia pine was simply the horridest wood in all the world, while, upon the other hand, Uncle Si speedily came to regard Alice as an arch enemy who was seeking to trick and impoverish him. The neighbors sided with Alice, of course. They freely expressed the conviction that Uncle Si and all other contractors would bear constant watching. It is perhaps needless for me to add that Uncle Si regarded all neighbors as impertinent and mischievous intermeddlers.

I will confess that of all the workmen about the place the plumbers interested me most. They came late and quit early, and much of the intervening time was spent in asking one another questions and in ordering one another about. No tool was at hand when it was required. If the pliers were needed the whole gang of plumbers stopped work to hunt for the missing instrument,

which was sometimes found in one remote
spot and sometimes in another — never
where it should have been. I have a theory
that for reasons best known to themselves
plumbers make a practice of mislaying and
losing their tools.

I supposed that having once begun their
work these plumbers would push it to com-
pletion. I never undertake anything that I
do not keep at it until it is done and finished,
and I think that this rule obtains among most
of the professions and trades. Plumbers
seem, however, to be a privileged class.
They come to your premises and spend an
hour or two examining what is to be done;
then they go away. When they get ready
to come back they return — this time with
a miniature furnace and whatever tools they
do not require. Then they go away to
bring the tools they need, leaving the tools
they do not require for a pretext for another
trip. Then they take turns at suggesting
how the proposed work should be done,
and one after another they get down upon
their knees and peer into closets and holes
and under floors and into dark places, after

which some of them go back to the "shop," for more things, while the others either sit around doing nothing or busy themselves at losing and mislaying the tools they have already at hand.

Uncle Si, who is an authority on the subject, says that there never was a plumber who died of overwork or in the poorhouse. He tells me that he once knew of a plumber named Bilkins who fell dead of heart disease one day when he discovered that he had worked four minutes overtime.

The boss painter was another individual who excited my astonishment. I never knew another man so fertile in the art of prevarication. Mr. Krome would rather lie than eat — at any rate, he would rather lie than paint. He never neglected to come over twice a day and take a long and careful survey of the house.

"I reckon you're about ready for us, eh?" he'd ask.

"We're waiting on you," Uncle Si would say.

"Then I'll have to put my gang at work in the mornin'," he would answer. This performance was repeated again and again, but the "gang" we looked for did not come. I remonstrated against this seeming neglect, but Mr. Krome blandly assured me that when his men did once get to work they would push the job with incredible speed. I knew he was a liar, yet I always believed the fellow.

We gave him the glazing to do. We even accommodated him to the extent of sending the window frames to his shop instead of making him haul them himself. We did this out of no special regard for Mr. Krome, for, aside from pure selfish considerations, Mr. Krome is no more to us than we are to Hecuba; but we desired to facilitate him in the work he had engaged to do for us.

After the window frames had been at the fellow's shop a fortnight, I began to suggest that their return would gratify me to the degree of rapture. Mr. Krome put us off with one excuse and another (all equally plausible) and presently a month had rolled by. Like the man in the fable who tried brickbats when kind words were no longer of avail, I threatened to turn the work of glazing over to another glazier who was not so busy with his lying as to prevent him from attending to the duties of his legitimate trade. This served as a mild remedy, for the window frames presently began to arrive one at a time, and I actually felt like calling upon our pastor for a special service of praise and thanksgiving when finally those windows were all in place.

The one thing that Alice, the neighbors, Uncle Si, and I were amicably agreed upon was the opinion that Mr. Krome, for a boss painter, was not worth the powder to blow him off the face of the earth. I felt tempted to tell him so, but he was at all times so amiable and so chatty that I really could not find the heart to mention a matter likely to interrupt the flow of his good nature. The chances are that Mr. Krome entertained much the same opinion of Uncle Si that Uncle Si had of Mr. Krome. My somewhat intimate association with workingmen for the last three months enables me to say that, so far as I have been able to observe, workingmen often have a precious poor opinion of one another. The plumbers talk of the carpenters as lazy and shiftless, the painters speak ill of the plumbers, the carpenters regard the tinners with derision, and so it goes through the whole category.

Now that I come to think of it, I am compelled to admit that this practice of setting a low estimate upon the endeavors and responsibilities of others is not restricted to the workingman's class. I blush to recall how often I myself have envied the apparent ease with which Belville Rock and Bobbett Doller stem the tide of human affairs while I labor on and on, barely eking out a subsistence. So far as I can see, they toil not, neither do they spin.

The chances are, on the other hand, that both Belville Rock and Colonel Doller regard me as the luckiest of lazy dogs, who has but to lie on his back and look at sun, moon, and stars to earn both fame and fortune. The farmer's candid conviction is that the city man is a fellow who does nothing and gets rich at it; the urban resident is quite as positive that the farmer habitually loafs around and lets God do the rest. The truth of this whole matter is that all humanity is prone to discontentment of that kind which not only denies happiness to oneself but also begrudges others the happiness they achieve.   ·

But of this frailty I shall speak no further; indeed, I do not understand how I happened to be led into this line of discourse, for it is quite at a tangent with the subject I had in mind — namely, the butler's pantry.

XXII

THE BUTLER'S PANTRY

IN the good old days, which were, of course, the days when you and I were boys and girls together at Biddeford, Me., our civilization knew nothing of that miserable invention which is now foisted upon the modern house under the name of butler's pantry. In those good old days we used to have pantries and china closets and butteries and all that sort of thing, and people were contented.

At the present time, however, civilization is so curiously possessed of a desire to ape the customs of European society that every kind of innovation is seized upon with enthusiasm and without any apparent regard for the derision and contempt to which it renders us liable. In my opinion (which is sustained by such an eminent authority as Lawyer Miles) the butler's pantry without the butler is as absurd a contrivance as a carriage without a horse or a purse without gold or silver to put therein. Yet there is not, I presume to say, a tenement house in all this city that has not its butler's pantry; without this adjunct no home is considered complete, and it makes no difference whether " the lady of the house " does her own work or is able to employ female servants, the butler's pantry is a sine qua non.

I told Alice that I regarded a butler's pantry much in the light of a last year's bird's nest, and I added that since we were going to have a butler's pantry minus the butler I supposed the next move would be in the direction of a wine cellar minus the wine. But my humor is wholly lost upon Alice; since she began training with other householders that superior woman has exhibited a strange indifference to my suggestions and counsel.

I mentioned Lawyer Miles a moment ago. This gives me the opportunity of saying that my sympathies have gone out with enthusiasm toward that gifted man ever since I heard him remark, not very long ago, that he liked to have things cluttered up in his house. I am not able to define the compound "cluttered-up," but it conveys to my mind a meaning that is perfectly clear, and it suggests conditions which are pleasing to me. I, too, like to have things cluttered up. The most dreadful day in the week is, to my thinking, Friday — not because we invariably have fried fish upon that day, but because it is upon Friday that a vandal hired girl appears in my study and, under the direction of my wife, proceeds to "put things in shape." Alice insists that I am not orderly or methodical, yet amid all the so-called disorder of my study I can at any moment lay my hands upon any chart or map or book or paper I require, provided everything is left just where I drop it.

My doctrine about such things is that books and charts and papers were made for use and are therefore of the greatest utility when most available. When I am at work I like my tools around me; if they are not handy, my work is interrupted, and an interruption often breaks the train of thought and renders impotent or at least mediocre an endeavor which elsewise would be excellent. In their ambition to "put things in shape," and to give me an object lesson in order and method, Alice and her vandal hired girl hide my tools of trade, disposing of my books, papers, and pens, and even of my slippers, in such ingenious wise as to keep me busy for hours finding these necessities and replacing them where they will be available.

I thought that Alice and her mercenary were the only women in the world addicted to this weekly practice, but from what Lawyer Miles and other married men tell me I gather that there are other wives in the world quite as possessed of the seven devils of order and method as Alice is.

To return to that other matter: Alice has hinted to me that she intends to store a great deal of my own porcelain and pottery away in the butler's pantry. I had hoped that when we got into the new house we should have plenty of space for displaying the platters, plates, bowls, teapots, etc., etc., to which age has added a special charm, and the collection of which has involved the expenditure of much time and money upon my part.

I am convinced, however, that Alice intends to hide all these beautiful old specimens away; the butler's pantry is evidently for this purpose. I have not questioned Alice about it, but (to use Uncle Si's favorite expression) "it 's dollars to doughnuts" that Alice is figuring on displaying her sixty-dollar set of new porcelain in the new glass cabinet in the dining-room, while my rare antiques — among them the blue platter, which was sent me from New Orleans, and which belonged originally to the pirate Lafitte — are relegated to the dim mysterious shelves of the butler's pantry, where dust will obscure them and spiders make them their favorite romping grounds. I intend to ask Lawyer Miles what he would do under like circumstances.

There is a sink in the butler's pantry, but it is wholly superfluous. I am told that this adjunct is useful in washing such dishes and glassware as are too precious to be sent to the kitchen. All this sounds very fine, but the practice is to whew the tableware of all kinds into the kitchen, whether there be a sink in the butler's pantry or not. My grandmother (and my mother, too) never suffered a servant to wash the fine porcelain or the cut glass; that responsible task was always reserved for the housewife herself, and the result was that no porcelain was chipped and no cut glass cracked. They sent me an old willow teapot from Biddeford, and it had n't been with us three weeks before our Celtic cook marred its symmetry by chipping off its venerable nozzle.

The only reason why so many charming bits of china have come down to us from the last century is that our grandmothers and our mothers cared for these things and protected them from rough usage. But, bless your soul! do you suppose Alice could be induced to bare her arms and apply herself to the task of washing a stack of antique porcelain or a row of cut-glass tumblers? No, not for the entire wealth of Wedgewood or the combined output of Dresden and of Sèvres!

Mrs. Baylor tells me that I am doing the butler's pantry a grave injustice; that the servants will use it, and that it will prove a great convenience. I do not wish to appear unreasonable and I am willing to concede that the servants will utilize the pantry and its death-dealing sink. It is very probable that under their auspices the slaughter of china and of glassware will be continued; it moots not to the average hired-girl whether the sink be in the kitchen or the butler's pantry, upon the housetop or in the bowels of the earth; the work of destruction goes on at four dollars a week and every Thursday out.

It was during the pantry agitation that Mr. Patrick Devoe came into our lives. He approached us one sweltering afternoon and introduced himself with all the urbanity of a native of Glanmire, County Cork. He praised our house and our premises and my wife and our children. We wondered what he was driving at, but he didn't keep us in suspense very long, for he was, as he assured us, a business man from the word "go." He was, it appeared, the proprietor of a street-sprinkling cart, and the object of his call upon us was to crave the boon of sprinkling Clarendon Avenue in front of our place at the merely nominal price of ten cents a day.

Mr. Devoe could hardly have called at a time more favorable to his interests. The day was, as I have already intimated, oppressively hot: there was a stiff wind from the south and the dust rolled up the avenue in clouds. Mr. Devoe represented to us that the other people in the neighborhood had contracted for his services and our reputation belied us if we were unwilling to secure at a paltry financial outlay what would contribute to our comfort and health. This persuasive gentleman assured us that, under the benign influence of his sprinkling cart, Clarendon Avenue would presently become one of the most popular of suburban driveways. Hither would equipages come from every quarter, and the thoroughfare eventually would be famed as the coolest, shadiest, and most fashionable in Chicago.

Furthermore Mr. Devoe represented that the trees, shrubbery, and grass of our premises would be directly benefited by his sprinkling cart; the gracious flood of water, distributed twice a day by his itinerant cart, would not only lay the dust of the highway, but also permeate and circulate through the contiguous soil, bearing refreshment and health to tree, plant, and flower alike. The vigor of vegetation meant much to humanity; by this means an abundance of ozone would be supplied to the circumambient atmosphere, insuring healthful sleep and general reinvigoration to man, woman, and child.

Mr. Devoe's presentation of the facts and possibilities was so convincing that both Alice and I recognized the propriety of securing his services. The sum of ten cents per diem seemed very trifling; it was not until after Mr. Devoe had departed with our contract in his pocket that we began to realize that, however insignificant ten cents per diem might be, seventy cents per week was not to be sneezed at, while twenty-one dollars for the season was simply a gross extravagance. I was in favor of recalling and annulling our contract with Mr. Devoe, but Alice insisted that we should keep strictly in line with the other neighbors, doing nothing likely to stigmatize us either as mean or as unfashionable.

A day or two after this incident a ruffianly looking fellow called on us to "make arrangements," as he said, about hauling away our garbage when we got moved into our new house. I told the fellow that the city sent a garbage wagon around every week to remove the garbage free of cost. To this the fellow replied that the city did its work carelessly, that the wagon was invariably overloaded, and that no reliance could be placed upon the garbage boxes being emptied if that responsible duty were intrusted to the city employés.

The fellow seemed to know what he was talking about, and his representations were so fair that finally I agreed to pay him twenty-five cents a week for hauling the garbage away. That evening I heard from Mr. Baylor that the scheme was a vulgar bit of blackmail; that the fellow was driver for one of the city wagons and made a practice of extorting fees from householders for doing work which he was already paid to do. I felt grievously outraged and I threatened to report this infamy to the municipal authorities. But Mr. Baylor and other friends assured me that these infamous practices of blackmail were encouraged at the City Hall, and that I would simply be laughed at if I ventured to complain.

It was about this time, too, that I paid a man four dollars to clean out the catch basin in the rear of our premises. The man told me that the catch basin was "reeking with the germs of disease." I did n't see how that could well be, since the sewer had not been laid six weeks. However, the man insisted, and he talked so portentously of bacteria and bacilli and morbiferous microbes that finally in a terror of apprehension I gave him four dollars and bade him do his saving work and do it quickly.

When the neighbors heard of this incident they unanimously pronounced me a fool, accompanying that opprobrious stigmatization with an epithet which my religious convictions prohibit me from recording.

XXIII

ALICE'S NIGHT WATCHMAN

FROM what I have already told you it is likely that you have gathered that Alice and I had good reason to conclude that being a householder was by no means as cheap an enjoyment as could be conceived of. We recalled the words of the sagacious and prudent Mr. Denslow. "When you get a place of your own," said that wise man, "you will find that there will be a thousand annoying little demands for your money where now there is one." Our other friend, Mr. Black, had expressed the same idea when he told us that "a house-owner never gets through paying out." If Alice and I had had any thought upon the matter at all it was to the effect that when we had a home of our own we got rid forever of the monstrous bugaboo of house-rent at sixty dollars a month. We supposed that all our spare time could be devoted to counting the money we were going to save by getting out of a grasping, avaricious landlord's clutches. Experience is a severe teacher; Alice and I have found out a great many things since we began to have direct dealings with builders, masons, plumbers, painters et id omne genus, as well as with sprinklers, day laborers, landscape gardeners, fruit-tree peddlers, lightning-rod agents, and others of that ilk.

We duly became aware that we were losing a good deal at the hands of nocturnal depredators. Our flower beds were despoiled with amazing regularity; the broken lath and old lumber which had been piled up in the back yard, and which Alice intended to use eventually for kindling, disappeared mysteriously, and the carpenters reported finding evidences every morning that some person or persons had been tramping through the house the night before.

We were all at once possessed of the paralyzing fear that this nocturnal trespasser, or these nocturnal trespassers, might set our house on fire. The floors were strewn with shavings; a spark would precipitate a conflagration, and the old Schmittheimer place would burn like so much tinder. I read over the fire-insurance policies which we had taken out with our genial friends, Doller, Jeems, and Teddy, and I found out that the companies represented by those gentlemen were not responsible for losses upon unoccupied premises, or for losses resulting from incendiarism. It occurred to me that it would be wise to invite the police to keep an eye on the place at night, but this plan seemed impracticable for the reason that I wanted to keep the lawn-sprinklers running all night in defiance of the ordinance, and this could not be done if the police were to be mousing about the premises.

While I was still worrying over this distressing problem one of the carpenters came to me with a harrowing tale about a tramp whom he had caught sleeping in the barn. This tramp had gained access to the barn by means of a window. He quietly removed the sash, after breaking the panes of glass, and crawled in. The carpenter caught the

impudent rogue early next morning in fla-
grante delicto — that is to say, found him
snoozing upon a mattress which Alice had
stored away in the barn for safe-keeping.
An argument ensued, but the tramp finally
beat a retreat.

Upon the evening of that same day the
carpenter remained after working hours to
see whether the tramp would come back for
another night's lodging in the nice, warm
barn on that nice, clean mattress. Surely
enough, as evening shadows fell the tramp
made his reappearance and sought to effect
an entrance to the barn. Thereupon the
belligerent carpenter emerged from his hiding
and bade the trespasser be gone. The tramp
complied with this demand, but not until he
had signified his intention of returning later
at night for the purpose of squaring accounts
with the carpenter.

This dark threat filled the carpenter with
gloomy forebodings and he hastened to
Alice and me for advice. Of course we assured him that we would support him in
any line of action he would take, and we
promised to pay him one dollar if he would

stay and guard the premises that night. The carpenter was not insensible to the soothing influences of lucre, and he consented to watch and defend our property, provided we furnished him with a weapon of one kind or another, for he had a conviction that the tramp fully intended to come back that very night to cut his heart out.

My acquaintance with weapons is limited to that circle which includes my collection of antique armor and several old flintlocks picked up at different times in New England and in the South. I confessed to the carpenter that I had in the house nothing suited to his bellicose purposes, unless he was willing to put up with a mediæval battle axe or a Queen Anne musket. The carpenter seemed disinclined to place any reliance upon these means of defence, and he suggested that perhaps I might borrow a pistol of some one of the neighbors. I had not thought of that before; the idea impressed me favorably, and I proceeded to act upon it. It was no easy task, however, finding what I wanted. At the Denslows an axe was the only weapon to be had, and at the Baylors', the Crowes', the Sissons', and the Ewings' I found that the spears had been beaten into plowshares and the swords into pruning-hooks. I felt that it would be folly to apply at the Tiltmans', for Jack Tiltman is the mildest man in seven States, and he is descended from a line of Quakers religiously opposed to war and strife. However, meeting with Tiltman, I ventured to confide to him the dilemma I was in, and I was surprised when he told me that he could provide me with any kind or size of revolver I wanted. Presently he brought out of his house a machine which, had he not assured me to the contrary, I should at first sight have mistaken for a one-inch aperture telescope.

"Is it loaded?" I asked.

"Yes, seven times," said he.

"And will it go off seven times all at once?" said I.

"Once will be enough," said he; and then he added that the bore was so large that if the bullet once struck a man it would let daylight clean through him, even in the night time.

You can well understand that. by the time

the carpenter was equipped for defensive operations, the whole neighborhood was worked up to a condition of great excitement. The children were enthusiastic over the prospect of bloodshed, and from the chatter that was indulged in by these innocents you might have supposed that a murderous tramp lurked at every corner. Alice and I walked over to the Schmittheimer place with the carpenter, and we were accompanied by several of our neighbors and their offspring. The evening was now advanced to the degree of darkness, and our heated fancies transformed every shadow into a living creature. Little Annie Ewing was on the verge of hysterics and declared she saw things behind every tree and stump, and Mr. Denslow contributed to the general excitement by recalling that he had read that very day of several mysterious murders down in a remote corner of Arizona by unknown tramps.

I admit that I, too, was much perturbed. I contemplated with indignation the lawless impudence of the fellow who had broken into our barn, and who had subsequently threatened violence to the carpenter for expostulating against this act of trespass. At the same time I could not stifle a feeling of pity for the homeless being who doubtless found the bed upon our barn floor as grateful as the downy couch of a Persian potentate. Nor could I stifle the conviction that it was a piece of miserable greediness on my part to deny this friendless and penniless wanderer the humble shelter he craved.

In fact I presently became so ashamed of the part I was taking in these proceedings that but for my regard for Alice's feelings I would have packed the carpenter off home and left the barn open to the tramp and all his kind. As it was my conscience gave me no rest until I had induced neighbor Tiltman to extract the cartridges from the pistol, which service he did so cleverly that the carpenter knew nothing about it, and continued to bluster and bloviate like a dragoon on dress parade.

The tramp did not return that night, and I was glad he did not, for it would have spoiled our new premises for me had any act of violence been committed thereupon. The experience, however, alarmed Alice to such an extent that she determined to employ a private watchman to guard the premises by night until we occupied them. She told me at supper the next evening that for this purpose she had secured the services of a poor but honest man who had called that day seeking employment.

"You don't mean to tell me, my dear," said I, "that you have intrusted this responsible duty to a person who is in the habit of travelling from house to house, asking alms!"

"I guess I know an honest man when I see him," said Alice, "and I know this man is honest, if there is such a thing as an honest man."

Alice went on to say that her protégé was an old soldier; that he had wept when he told of his unrequited services for his country, and of the ingratitude which he had experienced when his application for a pension was denied by the unfeeling authorities at Washington. Alice said she had never met with a more civil-spoken person, and he must indeed have impressed her most favorably, for she advanced him fifty cents on account.

We slept securely that night, for Alice's assurances made me confident that under the

new watchman's sleepless vigilance all would
be safe on the Schmittheimer premises. But
about seven o'clock next morning there was
a rude outcry, and there came a terrible
banging at our front door. Looking out into
the street we saw the carpenter with a very
sorry specimen of manhood in custody. The
carpenter was flourishing neighbor Tiltman's
unloaded pistol and threatening to blow his
prisoner's brains out.

"I caught him asleep in the barn!" cried
the carpenter, excitedly.

"Stop! Stop!" shrieked Alice. "Don't
shoot him! Don't harm a hair of his head!
He is the night watchman I hired to guard
the place!"

"He's the tramp!" insisted the carpenter.
"He's the very tramp who broke into the
barn and slept there once before. I 've
caught him now and I won't let him go!"

The prisoner protested that the carpenter
was mistaken, that he was, indeed, the night
watchman, and that he was entitled to "the
kind lady's protection."

The fellow's voice sounded familiar and I
recognized his form and face. Yes, there

could be no mistake; I had seen and dealt with this person before.

"My friends," said I, addressing Alice and her carpenter and the crowd of neighbors that had assembled, "you are right, and yet you are wrong. I know this man, and I identify him as the base ingrate who stole my new wheelbarrow and my garden utensils. Your name, sir," I continued, sternly, transfixing the quaking wretch with a glance of commingled anger and scorn, "your name is Percival Wax!"

XXIV

DRIVEWAYS AND WALL-PAPERS

HAD we been so disposed we could have given the wretched Percival Wax a great deal of trouble. Lawyer Miles was anxious to prosecute the fellow, and I dare say he felt that he had missed the greatest opportunity of his life when Alice and I concluded to let the matter drop. We were moved to this decision by the consideration that, while we owed Percival Wax only our resentment and vengeance, a prosecution of him for his numerous misdemeanors would put us to no end of trouble. The exposure and punishment of vice would doubtless prove much more popular among the virtuous, did not these proceedings involve so great an expenditure both of time and of labor. Alice and I were not long in making up our minds that we had plenty of other unavoidable troubles to engage our atten-

248

tion; so we let the tramp go, but not, however, until I had lectured him seriously upon the propriety of his abandoning his evil ways and until Alice had given him a clean shirt and an old pair of shoes with which to start out afresh upon the pathway of reform, which he solemnly promised to follow.

If you have ever passed the old Schmittheimer place — and doubtless you have, for it is the pride and ornament of a most aristocratic section — you must have noticed the roadway that leads from the street to the residence that looms up majestically two hundred feet back from the street. Perhaps you have wondered why grounds in other respects so attractive should be defaced by a feature so unsightly and so impracticable as this identical roadway.

And yet, as I told Alice, this roadway was actually the most natural feature of the place; there was absolutely no touch of artificiality about it; it was originally a stretch of sand, and such it had remained from time immemorial, by which I mean from that remote date — presumably eighteen centuries ago — when the receding waters of Lake Michigan left the spot subsequently to be known as the old Schmittheimer place high and dry in section 5, range 16, township 3. The genius of man had wrought wondrous and beautiful changes elsewhere, converting marshes into boulevards and transforming sandy wastes into blooming gardens; but never had it expended a touch or a thought upon that bald prehistoric streak which served as a driveway for all vehicles that dared invade the old Schmittheimer place.

How many vehicles had in the lapse of years been hopelessly maimed or totally wrecked while trying to traverse that roadway I shall not presume to say, for as a man of science I glory in exactness and I eschew surmise. This much I know, for I have seen it time and again during the last four months: nothing that moves on wheels has ventured upon that roadway that it did not sink slowly but surely up to the hubs of its wheels in the unresisting sand. The Pusheck grocery cart broke a spring the first time it drove in, and the wagon that hauled the steam fixtures was stalled for three hours in one of those treacherous depressions in which

the roadway abounds, depressions which,
as I am told, are known to dwellers in hilly
country places as " thank-ye-marms."

Until I became acquainted with this particular roadway I never fully comprehended
the nicety and the force of the phrase "to
drive in." I had heard people say that they
had driven into such and such places, and I
had wondered why they employed this figure
of speech when, it seemed to me, it would
have been more exact to say that they entered
upon or drove over. But I know now that
it is no figure of speech when one says that
he drives into the old Schmittheimer place.
No other phrase could more exactly express
an actuality.

If we were going to retain the driveway
in all its unhampered prehistoric simplicity,
just as the glacial period found and left it, it
would really be the proper thing for us to
found and to maintain a rescue station in its
vicinity, for we have been called upon to
hasten to the relief of every vehicle that has
" driven into " the premises since we took
possession. And a very serious theological
aspect of this matter is had in a considera-

tion of the fact that this prehistoric driveway not only breaks spokes and tires and hubs and springs, but also incites human beings to break the third commandment. I have overheard the young man who drives Pusheck's grocery cart indulging in expletives which I am sure he never learned as a member of Alice's Bible class.

So, taking one consideration with another, Alice and I determined to have a new road. Undoubtedly this was a wise determination; if we had gone ahead from that wise beginning and built the road as we had planned, all would have been well. The serious error we made was in seeking the counsel of our neighbors — the very same error we have made and kept on making over and over again ever since we entered upon this scheme of the new house.

I take it for granted that you know as well as I do that when it comes to roads, there are as many different kinds of roads as there are planetoids in the solar system. Furthermore, paradoxical as it may appear, each of these different kinds is better than any of these others, for each possesses not only all the advantages of the others, but also certain distinct and paramount advantages of its own. Alice and I had decided upon a dirt road, because we believed that a dirt road would conform in appearance to the other rustic and farmlike features of the place, and because we fancied that a dirt road could be constructed cheaply.

I use the term "dirt road" under protest. I am aware that what is called a dirt road is, properly speaking, an earth road. Dirt is filth, but earth is not; so when we call an earth road a dirt road we commit a vulgar error by employing a wrong epithet. All this I know, and yet, conforming to a custom, because it is a custom followed by all except a smattering of purists, I humiliate my sense of integrity, and I prostitute the virtue of my native speech.

In an unguarded moment, as I have intimated, we confided to our neighbors the precious secret that the stretch of sand from our front gate to our backyard was to make way for a modern, safe, and comfortable driveway. Immediately we were overwhelmed with suggestions and advice as to the particular kind of driveway we really ought to have. You may have noticed that whenever a friend (a dear, good friend) advises, he or she invariably tells you what you really *ought* to have — putting much emphasis on the "ought." This clinches and rivets the advice. When one says to you that you really *ought* to have such or such a thing, he means, of course, that you would have it if you were not either too poor or too stupid (or both) to get it. Alice and I are poor in purse, but I deny that we are idiots.

Not to consume your time with further discourse upon this subject (although I will concede that it has its fascinations and its importance), I will say that the primitive roadway (illustrative of the pre-glacial period) still winds its Saharan course through our premises. For Alice and I are undetermined whether to follow our own instincts and have a dirt road (there it is again!) or whether to concede to neighborly influence in the matter of this driveway, just as we have conceded upon nearly every other detail that has come up for consideration within the last four months. I dare say we shall eventually come back to our original plan, for it is already as clear as the noonday sun that if we adopt the suggestion of any one neighbor we shall have all the rest of our neighbors down on us for the rest of our lives.

We had an unpleasant experience of this character in the matter of wall-paper. It seems that Alice and Adah consulted all the women-folks in their acquaintance, and after much agitation made such selections of wall-paper as they believed would serve as a felicitous compromise between all parties consulted and all tastes expressed. The result is that nobody is suited —nobody but me. As for me, I am too much of a philosopher and too busy with my philosophy to spend any time worrying about the color or the pattern of the paper on the walls. If the paper is not so prepossessing as it might be, I should be glad that it is upon my walls rather than upon the walls of those whom it would vex much more than it does me.

I do not mind telling you that my favorite color in wall-paper (as well as in everything else) is red, and it was a delicate concession upon Alice's part to cover the walls of my

study over the kitchen with paper of unde-
niably red hue, upon which appear tracings
of yellowish white in a pattern particularly
pleasing to my uneducated eye. Little Josephine's room (which is shared by Alice's
sister Adah) is decorated with wall-paper in
which red is also the predominant color.
The pattern is of bunches of roses in full
bloom, and these counterfeit presentments
are so true to the life that when little Josephine first entered the apartment she reached
out her tiny hands in rapture and sought to
pluck the beautiful flowers. Adah, too, is
delighted with this floral design; the rose is
her favorite flower, and by a charming coincidence it happens to be also the favorite
flower of Adah's friend Maria — of course you
remember Maria; married Johnnie Richard-
son, and lives at St. Joe, Missouri. So, you
see, there are several tender sentiments attach-
ing Adah to that rose-bedecked apartment.

And yet (will you believe it?) there are
those who do not at all approve of the wall-
paper in which I and little Josephine and
Adah (to say nothing of Maria) take so great
delight. Some of these people have been

ill-mannered enough to laugh aloud and long when they beheld the impassioned hue of the covering of the walls in my study! There was one person (I forbear mention of her name) who seriously said she thought we 'd be afraid to let little Josephine sleep in that rose-garlanded room; that the glaring colors would be likely to give the dear child the " willies." I do not know what the " willies " are, but I do know that little Josephine sleeps well, eats well, and is happy, and this is all that we could hope for in one of her tender years.

Now while I cannot do otherwise than defend the choices in wall-papers which Alice and Adah have made, I distinctly recognize and I regret two very unpleasant facts : first, that by not complying with their advice upon the subject we have grievously offended a number of our neighbors, and. second, that Alice and Adah are prepared to set down in the list of their active and malignant foes every woman who presumes to disparage either by word or by look the wall-paper they have picked out as most pleasing to their tastes.

XXV

AT LAST WE ENTER OUR HOUSE

THE detail of hardware fixtures did not enter into our original calculations. This was very stupid of us, so everbody else said — everybody, of course, who had been through the ordeal of building a house. It is surprising how soon one who has had this experience forgets that before he had that experience he was as ignorant and as unsuspecting a body as could be imagined.

I suspect that after all it is a good thing for humanity that all people do not have to go through with what Alice and I have experienced the last four months. Otherwise the world would be filled with distrust, for I can conceive of nothing else so likely to sow the seeds of rancor and of suspicion in one's bosom as an experience at building a house.

It has seemed to me at times during the

last four months as if the carpenters and joiners and plumbers and painters were leagued against Alice and me to defraud and to rob us. I supposed that in these dull and hard times these people would feel in a measure grateful to us for giving them a chance to ply their trades. I find, however, that they expect me to be grateful to them for allowing me the privilege of paying them exorbitant prices for very indifferent services.

Alice wanted to make a contract in every instance, but she was wheedled out of this by the eloquent representations of the sharpers to the effect that it would be much cheaper in the end to pay for the material used and so much per diem for the actual labor done. This looked reasonable enough, but the result was wholly in favor of the per-diem fellows. Our experience has convinced us that a mechanic who is working per diem will never make an end to his job so long as the appropriation holds out.

Of what use would our new house have been to us if the doors and windows and screens and blinds had not been supplied

with the fixtures required for their operation ?
We have very little worth stealing, and yet
I feel more secure if there are locks upon our
doors and if the windows are fastened down.
Uncle Si knew that we would need bolts and
locks and other similar hardware fixtures;
the neighbors, our busiest advisers, knew it,
too; yet nobody ever said booh about these
things to us. They fancied, forsooth, that
we would have by intuition the knowledge
which they had acquired by costly experience! And when we complained of the expense and trouble involved in the selection
and purchase of these extras, the intimation
that we were unreasonably idiotic was freely
bandied about by the very people who
should have sympathized with us.

The fixtures came late, too late for the big
storm. There being no bolt or any other
fastening to the north porch door, the wind
blew that door open and the rain descended
in torrents upon the hardwood floor of the
guest chamber. Next day it was apparent
that the floor was practically ruined. The
carpenters agreed that it would have to be
scraped and that it was very likely to swell

and spring out of place on account of the soaking it had suffered.

Hardwood floors may have their advantages: they ought to have, for they are a costly luxury and they are a great care. Owing to the few hardwood floors in our new house we were delayed moving into the place for many weeks. When Uncle Si and his cohort got through with them they were as billowy as the surface of the ocean.

The painters came to us one by one and apprized us in confidence that those floors were the worst they had ever seen. They said that the carpenters must have supposed that we wanted a toboggan slide instead of hardwood floors. This sarcasm rankled in our bosoms.

At this critical juncture Lansom Mansom, the cabinetmaker who had made our bookcases for us, came to our relief with the suggestion that he be employed to "go over" the floors and make them practicable. He advised the per-diem scheme, and with characteristic good nature we acceded to it. Thereupon this crafty and thrifty person set himself about this delectable task, which busied him five weeks at four dollars a day —a sum not to be sneezed at, I can tell you.

When the floors were scraped and stained and varnished it took two weeks for them to dry; meanwhile nobody was permitted to approach them. A favored few among our most intimate friends were graciously allowed to peer in at the shining floors from the porch outside, and it seemed very tedious waiting for the time to come when we could put those floors to the uses for which floors are undoubtedly intended.

When at last we *were* suffered to walk upon the floors an unlooked-for casualty came very near dashing to the ground the cup of joy which our pride had, metaphorically speaking, raised to our lips. Little Josephine, the most precious jewel in our domestic diadem, had never before had any experience with hardwood floors, and no sooner did she begin to dance and caper on that smooth and lustrous surface than the innocent little lambkin lost her footing and fell, sustaining so severe a shock as to render the services of a physician necessary.

This mishap confirmed me in my dislike for hardwood floors, and that dislike has increased steadily. Several other people have come very near breaking their necks by losing their balance on that treacherous surface, and I confess that I myself am compelled to exercise the art of a Blondin in order to maintain my equilibrium in those slippery places.

Alice has always argued that hardwood floors were particularly desirable for the reason that they did away with the expense and care of carpets. It is true that we are to have no carpets in the apartments where these hardwood floors have been laid, but these handsome floors simply emphasize and italicize a man's poverty unless they are dotted with rugs, and there is none so foolhardy as to deny that the average rug costs five times as much as the average carpet. And the care demanded by a hardwood floor is exacting, for that shining surface, upon which every spot of dust stands out so distinctly, must be gone over daily with a soft brush, and must be wiped up with a wet cloth at least thrice a week.

Moreover the utmost precaution must be practised lest the surface of the hardwood floor be scratched or be seamed by the nails in one's boots or by the legs of tables or of chairs. Our youngest son, Erasmus, complains grievously of the restrictions put upon him since he entered upon this hardwood-floor epoch of his career. It is hard for the buoyant lad to understand why he is not to be permitted to slide and skate on these floors as he has hitherto been permitted to slide and skate on the floors of the rented houses we have lived in. I have not chided Erasmus for his remonstrances, for I, too, have been tempted to rebel against the new order of things. If either Erasmus or I ever build a house of our own we shall eschew the hardwood-floor heresy as we would a pest.

There is another evil which I am at this moment reminded of, and that is the folding-door evil. In all my experience I have never met with another door as honest, sensible, and trustworthy as the door that swings on hinges.

I told Alice so when the subject of doors came up in our discussions of proposed innovations in the new house. But Alice had conceived the notion that we ought to have a folding door in the parlor, and when Alice once gets a notion into her head all creation with a pickaxe couldn't get it out again.

Properly speaking, the door was not a folding door; it was a sliding door. When pushed back it was to disappear in the wall separating the parlor from the front hall. When I saw Uncle Si and his men constructing this door I expressed the fear that it wouldn't work, but Uncle Si laughed my fears to scorn; the trouble with too many doors, he said, was that they were made of cheap stuff; *this* door, he assured me, was an A No. 1 door and would never — could never — get out of place. Then he showed me the rollers and attachments and proved their practicability and strength.

Not knowing any more about such things than a seacow knows of the summer solstice, I assented to all his propositions and went my way with my apprehensions completely allayed. But in less than forty-eight hours after Uncle Si and his men turned over the house to us, bang went that door, and no power at our command could budge it an inch either way.

Another carpenter came and investigated. Presently he shook his head and smiled a bitter smile. Then he told us that the break would not have happened if the fixtures had not been of the cheapest make. What we required, he said, was fixtures that cost ten dollars instead of three dollars, our door being a large parlor door and not a light pantry door.

We bade this sarcastic genius go ahead and remedy the evil as best he could, and the result is that the door now slides as smoothly as even the most exacting could wish: this repair has involved the expenditure of only fifteen dollars, and I would not mention it if I had any confidence whatever in the door even in its rehabilitated condition. I know as well as I know anything else that as soon as we build a fire in our heating apparatus next November the heat thereof will warp and twist that door into such shape that it will be as impossible to budge it as if it were nailed down. We shall then be in a serious pickle, for we shall be unable to enter our parlor.

The windows all over the house are fast in their casings, having been painted so carefully by those rascally painters that it requires the power of a steam derrick to raise them. The other morning I tried to open one of the windows in the butler's pantry, for the atmosphere in that place was absolutely stifling. I tugged and pulled and pushed in vain.

Finally a happy thought struck me, and I hunted up a hammer and used it lustily upon the obstinate sash. I must have got careless, for after I had hammered away for several minutes I missed my aim and the head of the hammer went through a pane of glass.

I didn't want Alice to know anything about this mishap, so I furtively hired a glazier to repair the damage I had done. As I made no contract with the fellow he took advantage of me. just as I should have known by experience he would. Here is a

copy of the bill he has just sent in for me
to pay:

"REUBEN BAKER, Esq., to J. SYKES, Dr.

To one pane glass 7x11.............................,...... .30
To one day's labor setting same $3.60

Total $3.90
Please remit."

[It was the intention of Mr. Field to add
a final chapter to his book describing the
entrance of the Baker family into their new
home, but his sudden death left the book
with this chapter unwritten.]

www.ingramcontent.com/pod-product-compliance
Lightning Source LLC
Chambersburg PA
CBHW030635030726
47497CB00006B/1806